Praise for

# *How to Get Arrested*

"A perfect balance between gritty and fun! *Arrested* leaves me dying to know what happens next."

> ~ V.S. Holmes, author of the Nel Bently Books and Reforged series

"An adventure worth starting!"

> ~ Amy Spitzfaden, author of *Untold*

"How to Get Arrested is a light read, entertaining and fast-moving, its dialogue flecked with idiomatic American dialect that lends it an air of authenticity."

> ~ J.C. Steel, author of the Cortii series and *Death Is For The Living*

Also by Cameron J Quinn

**THE STARSBORO CHRONICLES:**
*How to Get Arrested*
*How to Diagnose a Changeling**
*How to Stalk a Stalker**
*How to Defend a Damsel... Or Babysitter... Whatever*
*How to Get Kicked Out of School*
*How to Catch a Serial Killer**

**ANTHOLOGIES (CONNECTED TO STARSBORO)**
"How to Curse a Kingdom" *Out of the Darkness*
"How to Abduct an Alien" *Beamed Up*

**PARANORMAL ROMANCE**
Suckers in Love
*Vampire Viking in Vegas**

Bump in the Night
*Bite Me Once**

Tales from the Salem Grimoire
*Salem Witch**

**Forthcoming*

# How to Get Arrested

The Starsboro Chronicles:
Episode 1

## Cameron J Quinn

AMPHIBIAN PRESS

Amphibian Press
www.amphibianpressbooks.com
www.cameronquinnbooks.com
Cover by Aaron Bolduc
www.aaronbolduc.com

ISBN: 978-1-949693-93-5
First Edition

*Dedicated to my Readers,*

*Thank you for everything you do to keep me writing. Emails, reviews, and messages make all the difference.*

*Thank you!*

In *How to Get Kicked Out of School,* Trent is front and center. While Zurik and Morgan are off fighting a would be demon in Charlotte (How to Make a Monster), Trent finds himself face to face with a real demon in Starsboro. Not to mention the girl he has feelings for and her crazy ex's plot to get them kicked out of school.

Read *How to Get Kicked Out of School* for free at

**CameronQuinnBooks.com/freebook**

# ONE
# WHAT EVIDENCE?

Detective Jennifer Morgan watched the suspect through the one-way mirror as she swirled the ice in her coffee. He looked normal. Attractive, even, with his dark hair and tanned skin. But his eyes. Something about them sent a chill down her spine. He looked up from the cuffs on his wrists right at her. Those electric blue eyes pierced her soul. If she didn't know any better she'd think he could actually see her.

He shifted in his seat as he turned his attention back to the cuffs. She turned up the volume from the room and heard singing. She searched the lyrics on her phone. It was the opening lines from Volbeat's *Still Counting*. A smile spread across her lips. He was a cocky asshole.

"You think you can get a confession?" Captain Reynolds stood in the doorway behind her. His dark brown skin was slightly wrinkled around his eyes and forehead. His black hair was cut short and greying at the temples but the youthfulness in his eyes brought a smile to her face.

"He's rich so there's a good chance he thinks he's untouchable but I've always enjoyed a challenge. Who knows, maybe he'll hang himself with his grandfather's purse strings."

"Keep me posted, we had a robbery gone bad about an hour ago and Jefferson is bringing the suspects in."

"Cavazos will be back in a few, he just went to get decent coffee." She teased. Reynolds changed the coffee brand in an effort to save some money for new bulletproof vests but it was god awful. It tasted burnt no matter how fresh it was.

"Fine, next time I'll get the premium blend made from only the best beans, shit from only the best ocelots. I'll have to dock everyone's pay to buy the perfectly roasted tree nuggets but at least I won't have to hear how awful the coffee is anymore. And you can all die of gunshot wounds." he snapped.

"I'm only teasing," she smiled at him. "But seriously, no coffee is better than that coffee."

"Perfect. I'll save even more money next month when I don't buy any at all."

"You won't need too, there will still be plenty of that shit left I'm sure."

He waved her words off as he left the room. She looked back to her suspect. Then to the security photo she'd taken from the preowned video store's camera. There was no doubt about those piercing blue eyes. They were almost electric.

She steeled up, straightening her shoulders and put on her best bitch face before opening the door, file in hand.

She entered quickly, as if she'd been busy, looking at the file and sat at the table. She could see him sizing her up from across the steel surface in her peripherals. She hit record on the camera and looked at him. His band T was stretched across his chest and the rips in his jeans looked to be homemade rather than factory.

"Zurik D'Vordi?" she asked still not looking at him. "That's an interesting name."

"My mom liked to travel," his voice was low and gravely as a steady tck from the handcuffs hung in the air between them. Her body shivered as his voice slid over her. She shook her head to clear it. *He is a suspect*, she reminded herself.

She closed the file and looked him in the eye. His glare was unwavering making it hard for her to stare him down. Those damn eyes.

"I see you've called a lawyer, would you like to wait until they arrive?"

"No, I think we can clear this up before he gets here. Then I can take him out to dinner instead. That will be significantly more fun."

"Don't like our hospitality, Mr. D'Vordi?" she smiled.

"Not particularly fond of being tied up, at least when there's no bed involved."

"Do you know how many homicides your name came up in?" she snapped as the image of him naked and ready, strapped to her bed flew through her mind.

"I lost count," he smiled. Morgan felt a smile at the edge of her lips and fought it back. He was charismatic and his smile was contagious. He was probably a serial killer.

"Nine, in North Carolina and that's just the ones you were implicated in as a suspect. More if I include the ones you witnessed but were cleared for. That's a lot for a twenty-eight year old," she said. "And now that we've picked you up, congratulations Mr. D'Vordi, you've hit double digits."

"Had to happen eventually."

"Really? I've never been involved in any outside of work. In fact, I could argue most people aren't involved in any in their entire lives."

"When your job is protecting people from psychos, that raises the odds a bit." His eyes shifted to the mirror and she couldn't help but wonder if Cavazos was back with coffee.

"Yes, I see here you're employed by your Uncle? Lex M'Kray?" she held up his file.

"Yes ma'am," he sighed in irritation as he tipped his chair back on two legs.

"As private security?"

He nodded.

"Please speak your answer for the recording."

"Yes, that's correct, ma'am."

"So, who were you protecting when you killed the five men in front of the video store?" his face went pale as he set the chair back on all fours. She had him now.

"I beg your pardon?"

"We have security footage of you killing five men in front of Al's Discount Audio and Video. According to the time stamp, last night at about 9:30."

"Let's see it then."

"The footage?"

"Yeah," he said. His voice held the distinct edge of irritation.

"You don't have an alibi you'd like to offer up?"

"I was at home with my brother, who would lie to save my ass so that's off the table. There was the blonde later in the evening but I lost her number. Of course, she'll probably track me down in a day or two. You know how those things tend to go. You tell a chick you're not interested in the long term but she convinces herself she can change you after one night of incredible se—"

"Very well," she interrupted his tirade and stood to get the TV.

She let the door close behind her and moved to watch Zurik thought the window. He still didn't look too worried but his foot was bouncing and his hands were clenched together. She was starting to get to him.

"Video didn't rattle him as much as I thought it would." Cavazos' smooth baritone rolled over her with the promise of decent coffee and a second pair of eyes and ideas to crack this suspect.

Cavazos was about five feet ten with light brown skin. His voice held the slightest hint of a Texas lilt. His parents immigrated to the United States before he was born. Growing up in Texas, he'd joined the military to prove his patriotism making him the most multicultural all American boy she'd ever met.

"He's showing signs of distress. Once we show him the video it'll all be over. Just wanted to observe him for a moment." She took the coffee Cavazos offered and swirled it in her hand.

"He looks pretty cool to me."

She looked back at Zurik and he was relaxing with his head back slumped in the chair as if he might fall asleep.

"I guess he's decided not to worry yet."

"Can I ask you a question?" Cavazos asked before sipping his coffee.

"Of course."

"Why'd you come here?" It was the question she'd been dreading for the last six weeks. Her heart hammered in her chest. Anxiety threatening her carefully curated calm. "Not that I don't like having you and all your experience on my side but you seem like a go getter. You know, someone who'd thrive in the city."

"I needed a change of scenery." It wasn't exactly a lie. She'd left New York City for a whole slew of reasons. None of which were the sticky humidity and flat beige scenery of coastal North Carolina.

"You keep going. I'll hold back until it seems like we need to really put the screws to him."

"Alright," she grabbed the laptop and headed back into the interrogation room. Zurik laughed as she entered. "Something amusing?"

"No ma'am, just the idea that Starsboro PD could actually get enough evidence to arrest someone, never mind try the case."

She glared. She was use to suspects at least respecting the establishment she worked for. "I'm new here, but I promise, if you did this, I will not only find the evidence to arrest you, I will also see you thrown in a hole so deep you'll never see another living creature—or blonde—again."

There was an irritating glint in his eye as a half smile tugged at his lips. "You're feisty. I like that. They need people like you around here."

She felt something strange stirring in her. Butterflies? She cleared her throat to steady herself and turned on the computer.

The street outside the video store was lit up in the distinct green of a night vision camera as a group of teenaged girls walked by. Laughing and teasing each other as they went.

Morgan looked to Zurik. He was grinning from ear to ear. The resolution wasn't the best but she knew his face would show up clear enough.

Now a group of young men came into view and then a single man, who she knew to be Zurik, stepped in front of them and started attacking. One by one he severed their heads with a machete. Keeping his back to the camera until the very end. He would watch as the last one ran off and then look right at the camera.

Morgan felt her stomach drop. The film glitched before he turned his head and then went black.

"Alright, Benson, I don't know about you but I couldn't recognize any faces on that video. Let alone my ugly mug so do you have evidence from the bodies that somehow links to me?"

She paused. There was something about beautiful people calling themselves ugly that irritated her beyond rational thought. And the glint in his eye that said he knew the answer to his question pushed her nearly over the edge.

"The lab is working on the physical evidence now." she lied. There was no evidence. No bodies. Nothing. "What did you do with the bodies?"

"It could have been anybody." Zurik said with a smile. "It could have been you."

"We have reason to suspect you based on your height, weight, dress, and your lack of an alibi," she snapped. Someone in this building tampered with the tape. Things just went from bad to worse for the Starsboro PD.

"I didn't see me. And since I look at me more than you do I think I'd know."

She pulled the photo of him looking at the camera from the file and slid it across the table. "Whoever you had tamper with the tape forgot something."

He frowned at the image. Finally shaken.

"I want my lawyer."

"It sucks when you can't get away with murder doesn't it. Now, I want to know Mr. D'Vordi, why did you let the last one go?"

"It wasn't me, and I'm not answering another goddamn question until my lawyer gets here."

"Who is it?" Morgan asked. "I'll find out his ETA"

Zurik smiled a toothy grin and she felt her adrenaline pump into her veins. She couldn't get a decent read on this guy. "Jack Turner."

"His lawyer is Jack Turner?" Cavazos asked sounding defeated.

"Yeah, who is he? Some crooked defense attorney? He's obviously in D'Vordi's pocket. The guy's been to more crime scenes than I have."

"Turner is not only the best defense attorney in the state, he's also the one who starts charities and gets wrongfully convicted people out of jail pro bono."

"How?"

"He made a name for himself when he was pretty young and tried a lot of high profile cases. He made a lot of money, but I was thinking he must have been taking donations or something but maybe it's Zurik and his family on retainer."

"Right," she slumped down in her chair as she remembered Zurik's grandfather and his oodles and oodles of money. "Perfect."

"Well his grandfather would probably rather pay Turner when this shit pops up rather than deal with it himself.

"I'm sure Markus would love to hear the Starsboro Police Department think she's paying me to babysit." The man standing behind Cavazos was tall with dark brown skin and a tailored grey suit with a satin lavender tie. His hair was kept short but he had a thick beard that was starting to go grey on his cheeks. "I'd like to see my client now."

"Mr. Turner, I'm detective Jennifer Morgan--we haven't had the pleasure." Morgan held her hand out to him. He shook it and gave her a genuine smile that told her far more about his capabilities than Cavazos had. "Right in here."

As soon as they entered the room Zurik gave Turner a goofy grin followed a wave that showed off his handcuffs.

"Can we get the cuffs off of him, we're in an interrogation room, he won't be escaping."

"Why'd I call you then?" Zurik teased as Morgan slid the key in the cuffs.

"You'll be leaving very soon, Zurik don't worry about that. But in the meantime, I need you to stay quiet."

"I don't think so," Morgan asserted. She offered the photo to Turner.

"We'll need a moment."

As she left she heard Zurik speaking: "I know it looks bad, but you can't see shit on the actual video."

She sighed. He didn't act or sound guilty, but he didn't act or sound innocent either. Something weird was going on and she couldn't put her finger on what it was. She looked at Cavazos out in the bullpen typing away. And stuck her head out the door.

"What are you doing?"

"Getting the release papers ready and starting my report."

She slid up to him. Eyeing the work he was doing. "You're that certain our photo isn't going to matter?"

"He'll be out before the hour is up, Morgan." Cavazos said. "We'll continue to work the case, find more evidence. But he'll be back on the street tonight."

She crossed her arms over her chest. This wasn't justice. This wasn't how the system was supposed to work. They should be able to hold him at least. "Where's Reynolds?"

"He should be back in his office."

Without responding she headed up the three stairs to the offices. Sure enough he was on the phone yelling at someone about jurisdiction. When he hung up and slumped down into his chair she entered the office. He looked like he'd aged a decade in the last five minutes, she didn't want to tell him about the tape. She closed the door and approached his desk, determined to bring him up to date.

"More good news I assume?"

"You know me," she gave a fake laugh. "I only bring good news."

"What is it?"

"The D'Vordi case is going to be a real challenge." She gave him an exaggerated smile and raised her brows, nodding enthusiastically. He didn't move or react in any way. He just stared at her. She relaxed and came clean. "Someone tampered with the security footage. It cuts off just before Zurik looks at the camera."

He let out a heavy sigh, his eyes fell to his desk and he brought both his hands up to his face as if he were praying. "So we have a bigger problem than Zurik D'Vordi."

"I would say equally big, Sir." Morgan said shaking her head. "The way Zurik cut down those men. He'll do it again. We need to find the survivor before he does."

"You work on that, I'll try and find the compromised officer."

# TWO
# LET FREEDOM RING!

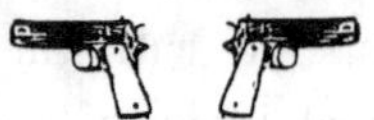

Zurik walked out of the police station into the humid North Carolina summer night and took a deep breath. Turner stood with Detective Jennifer Morgan by the door as the familiar roar of Zurik's 1969 Chevy Camaro indicated it's arrival. The car stopped at the curb, its red paint and white racing stripes making it unmistakable. Zurik's younger brother, Trent, stepped out of the driver's side as Zurik hopped over to the car to inspect it.

"Thanks for picking up my baby!" he said sliding a hand over the hood and inspecting the paint and tires. "I didn't like leaving her in that neighborhood."

"I got there just as they were putting it on the blocks."

"Are you serious?"

"No, Zurik. It was fine." Trent chuckled to himself as movement by the station doors drew Zurik's attention.

"You wanna grab a bite?" Zurik asked Turner as he approached. Detective Morgan watched with crossed arms. Zurik gave her one more once-over before offering Turner his full attention.

"Dude," Trent said smacking Zurik's shoulder. "Is that who arrested you?"

"Yeah."

"I would have told Jack to take his time if I'd known," Trent wagged a brow at him.

"She's gonna be the one to put me in jail. If I'm in with her, you tell Jack it's an emergency." Zurik laughed. He looked to the lawyer. "Dinner?"

"Yeah, I'll follow over."

"Frank's?" Trent suggested their favorite burger joint.

Turner nodded.

"See you there." Zurik winked at Morgan. The chances she wasn't going to tail him seemed slim.

Morgan poured over the crime scene report again. There were no bodies, no blood. Just ash. Tons of it everywhere. As if a crematorium exploded nearby.

She looked up from the report to Cavazos sitting at the desk across from hers. His face lit by the blue glow from his computer, the screen reflected in his glasses. It was clear he'd been pulling at his thick hair in frustration. A 5 o'clock shadow now covered his once cleanly shaven face.

"There aren't any bodies."

"Yeah, we knew that. He must have moved em." Cavazos said without looking up.

"The video didn't show him coming back. Moving anything."

"So, what does that mean?"

"I don't know."

Her phone buzzed on the desk and she grabbed it. The call was from Unknown. She frowned as she slid the green phone icon across the screen to answer it.

"Morgan," she said glaring at the evidence, or lack thereof, on her desk.

"Stop investigating Zurik D'Vordi."

"I beg your pardon?" she asked staring at Cavazos. He glanced at her then did a double take. She signaled for him to start a trace on the call, but he just shrugged.

"Stop the investigation. He's too important. We have it under control."

"Who's we?"

"People who are higher up on the ladder than you. That's all you need to know for now."

"That's not how this works pal," she said her tone angry. "You don't get to make demands. Not of the SPD and certainly not of me."

"You are a fireball aren't you."

"Go to hell." She tapped the little red phone icon as angrily as she could while silently wishing it was an old phone she could slam down and listen to the tiny bell ring out her anger.

"What the hell was that?"

"A scare tactic from our most recent playboy turned felon."

"Morgan?" Reynolds was leaning out of his office and made a motion for her to join him when they made eye contact. "You too, Cavazos."

They entered the office and the captain motioned for them to take a seat.

"I just got an interesting call from the director of the FBI."

Morgan and Cavazos exchanged a look.

"It seems our little investigation is stepping on some big toes."

"So they're trying to what? Make a case that he's a serial killer?" Morgan asked.

"Not quite. But the point is, our part in this is over. We need to finish our reports and drop the case. It won't be going to court."

"What?" Morgan snapped. "He can't get away with murdering those men."

"We have nothing," Reynolds said. "Those men don't have names, we can't find so much as a drop of blood let alone bodies. It's over Morgan."

"No. You can't stop us here. Those men might be nameless to us but to someone, they're husbands, fathers, sons. You cannot do this."

"It's out of my hands Morgan. Zurik will get what's coming to him. It doesn't matter if the case is made by us or the FBI."

Morgan stood with a huff and stormed out of the station. She was in her car and outside the liquor store before she even knew what she was doing. She stared at the neon OPEN sign and thought about the warm burn of a shot of Jack Daniel's whiskey. She sighed as she pulled her one-year sobriety coin out of her pocket and flipped it between her fingers.

"Not today." She started the engine and went in search of a red Camaro.

"Zurik," Trent said, trying to pull his brother's attention away from his burger. Zurik ignored him for the most part. "You need to take this seriously."

"I know, that Dick is out to get me," Zurik smiled at his pun.

"That *Dick* is serious. She's from New York and she's worked a lot of cases. Her close rate is—impressive." Trent stared at his phone as he scrolled through the information on Morgan. Trent was right as usual. The little buzz kill.

"Listen to your brother, Zurik. You need to lay low for a couple of days." Turner chimed in before putting a sweet potato fry in his mouth.

"You know I can't do that," Zurik's tone was deadly serious. "If I lay low, the fey snag their last couple girls and go into hiding for the next sixteen years. If I don't find them now, Vicky, Trisha, and Karly don't stand a chance."

"I'll hunt the fey, you need to be seen doing non-hunting type things," Trent said.

"No offense little bro, but this is pro stuff and as long as your focus is school--as it should be--you're all amateur."

"You can't save anyone if you're in jail," Turner said. "I can get that image thrown out but only because someone messed with the tape in the police station."

"What?" Zurik and Trent asked in unison.

"The image is from the original tape. You seem to have a guardian angel in the SPD but I wouldn't count on stuff like this happening again. Even if that person doesn't get caught this time, they may not feel like putting their neck on the line again."

"Then it's settled," Trent said. "I'll find the nest, you go to parties, be seen publicly with lots of pretty women. You know, do what you do."

"You want me to sleep around?" Zurik narrowed his eyes on his brother.

"The point isn't to break hearts, it's to be seen not murdering people."

"I can do that," Zurik said as he sipped his beer. "After I find the fey nest."

Turner and Trent exchanged a look like Zurik wasn't sitting right there. But at least he could tell they knew better than to argue any further.

"How are the girls?" Zurik asked Turner, looking for a more pleasant subject.

"They're doing well." Turner smiled. "Simone is applying to colleges. She'll be going to Yale of course. I still wish you'd let me put in a good word for you, Trent. Being an Alumni has a lot of pull in the Ivy League world."

"I still really appreciate the offer Jack, but I think I need to stay close to home."

Zurik glared at his little brother. He hated that Trent wouldn't go off to a good school. And hear that it was because Trent felt the need to babysit him made it worse.

"And Tasha?" Zurik asked.

"She's going a different path. I'm a bit worried actually."

"What do you mean?" Trent asked.

"She's withdrawn. Angry. And I'm worried about the people she's hanging out with."

"But she's not," Zurik started. Something strange hit him in the chest as the thought crossed his mind and it was hard to breathe. "Hunting?"

"Not yet," Turner said. His eyes lingered on Zurik. For the first time since they'd met a few years ago, Jack looked old.

"Is she researching?" Trent asked. "Have you checked the browser history on the computers and phones?"

"Yes, and I haven't found anything yet. I have a feeling she just knows how to cover her tracks in that department." Turner ran a shaky hand through his hair. "And she has access to computers at school, the library, you name it."

"Do you want me to talk to her?" Zurik asked. "I can come visit after this case."

"I'm not sure it will help but I'm willing to try anything. I truly appreciate what you guys do, but I don't want that life for my daughter."

"Neither do I," Zurik said. This wasn't a life. It was a death sentence. Zurik had an advantage. Being half immortal made it harder for him to lose the fight and evened the playing field with these things. Tasha was too young and vulnerable. Zurik met human hunters in the before. They always worked in groups. And they were tough, miserable people who needed alcohol and drugs to cope with all they'd seen--and done. That was definitely not the life for Tasha.

Zurik cut the engine as he pulled into his normal parking space. Their house was just off the Starsboro University campus, so Trent could take classes and Zurik could patrol the grounds for supernatural creatures out for a late night pre-law snack.

His gaze fell on the black Mercedes to the left of his spot.

"What's Markus doing here?"

"You know he hates when you do that," Trent said, stepping out of the car. "Just call him Grandpa and everything will go much smoother."

"What will go smoother?"

"Dude," Trent sounded exasperated. "You were arrested. Do you really need help putting these pieces together?"

"I was brought in for questioning, there's a difference."

"Sure, our million-year-old grandfather will totally get the 'difference'," Trent said, air quotes included.

"I'm not that old," Markus' gravely voice sent a chill down Zurik's spine even years after moving out on his own. "I'm barely one thousand and you're already gearing up to ship me off to a nursing home."

"I know Grampa," Trent said sounding ashamed. "I'm sorry."

Zurik shook his head at his pushover baby brother.

"To what do we owe the honor?" Zurik asked pulling a pack of cigarettes from his pocket. Markus glared. "I know it's hard for the owner of the company to step out. Even for family."

"Not when family is all over the police scanners," Markus said as he took the cigarette out of Zurik's mouth, snapped it in two, and threw it to the ground. "What happened?"

"Nothing I couldn't handle on my own."

"So I didn't see Jack Turner leaving the police station?"

"Gramps, why don't we talk about this tomorrow morning, at breakfast when we're all well rested?" Trent suggested.

"We will talk about it now," Markus growled. "Inside."

"What? Afraid the neighbors will hear you yelling and call Forbes?" Zurik chuckled.

"Inside."

Trent shot Zurik a look, begging him to cool it but Zurik had a nasty streak where his grandfather was concerned. They entered the small house and Zurik made his way to the kitchen. This interaction required alcohol. He leaned into the fridge only to remember he was supposed to pick up beer on the way home tonight.

"You let me forget the beer," Zurik said to Trent, his voice strained.

"Sorry I was a bit preoccupied."

"You don't need alcohol to talk to me," Markus snapped.

"I beg to differ."

"Zurik, this has to stop. You can't be running around town playing hero your whole life. You'll die alone in an alley somewhere. Old and alone."

"Maybe," Zurik said looking the old man in the eye. "If I age. We really don't know how that's going to go, do we?"

"We need to proceed like we do know. I don't want you to wake up one morning realizing you're aging and it's too late to turn your life around."

"I can't leave people to die when I have the power to save them."

"People die everyday Zurik. You can't save them all."

"Even if I only save one, its worth it. But that's the difference between you and me, isn't it? I save people, and you kill them." Zurik pushed past his grandfather and headed for the door. "I need a drink."

# THREE
# CHERRY LAND

"He didn't mean it." Trent gave a heavy sigh as the door slammed shut. "You just couldn't wait till tomorrow could you?"

"No, and I doubt it would have made much difference." Markus sat at the countertop looking older than Trent ever remembered. Most of his life, Markus was a tyrant king. Corrupted by the very magic he'd needed to save his kingdom, he hurt people for the pleasure of it until his son--Zurik and Trent's father--stopped him. But Markus had already killed his wife, That's why he traveled through a portal to North Carolina to live and die alone. Until his two grandsons and Lex M'Kray showed up on his doorstep. His black hair was almost completely gray and crow's feet surrounded his silver-blue eyes.

"He at least would have been home for the night. That detective is watching his every move and he's going to want to kill something before he comes back."

"I'm sorry Trent. I never know what to say where he's concerned."

"You can't, Zurik will never listen to you. Only the Gods know why, but he won't."

"I can't just watch him throw his life away."

"You don't have too. Call Lex next time. He listens to Lex."

"Maybe," The hurt in his grandfather's eyes made his chest tighten.

"I'm sorry Gramps. You raised us well," Trent said. "Zurik just has a chip on his shoulder."

"He remembers what it was like with your mother. I could never give him that kind of love. She was made to be a mom. Just like your grandmother. So patient and just content to be with you."

"I know. It wasn't easy on her either. Being so far away as we grew up."

"You should call her soon," Markus said. "Your mother and father have been calling more frequently hoping to catch either of you."

"I'll swing by tomorrow."

"Bring Zurik with you, maybe Marina can explain mortality better than I can. I've only been mortal for a few years now."

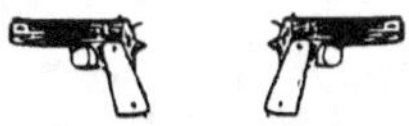

Morgan arrived at Cherry Land, the local hangout for the rougher patrons. The lot was almost full, but Zurik's Camaro was nowhere to be seen. The large neon cherries flashing in the window caught her attention.

She gave a heavy sigh, unsure what she hoped to find by tracking him down again. She knew Zurik was involved with these crimes, but she still needed new evidence. Something to make it so the FBI had to give the case back. She glared at the cherries for a moment before stepping out of her car. She should go home and settle in with the latest episode of *Game of Thrones* and a pint of Ben & Jerry's. Instead, she locked the car and made her way to the front doors of the establishment.

She sat at the bar and ordered a club soda, staring at the bottles of liquor displayed on the back of the bar. The bottle of Patron shimmered in the dim light. Or was that her imagination?

The female bartender followed her gaze as she dried a glass. She had long, honey-colored hair pulled back into a low ponytail and a leather vest that revealed more than it covered. Several tattoos were scattered about her bare shoulders and muscular arms that did not detract from her beauty.

"Can I get you anything?" she asked.

"I'm fine with the club soda, thank you," Morgan answered. Her voice was not as firm as it usually was. Her thoughts drifted back to her younger days on the force and why she gave up drinking in the first place. "Have you ever made a mistake so horrible that you couldn't forgive yourself?"

The bartender took a few steps toward her, frowning. "You're the only female cop, right?"

"That's me," Morgan said, laughing. "The only female Dick in the history of the department."

"I'm Shelly," the woman said, offering her hand. "I've made a lot of mistakes, but I can't say any have been so bad I would beat myself up for more than a week or two."

"I made the worst mistake a person can make." Morgan tipped the glass and swirled it on the bar as she spoke. "Because of me, my best friend is dead."

"I'm sorry for your loss." Shelly's words were genuine—more genuine than most.

"Don't worry about it," Morgan replied. Her tone was dead. "I need a shot of Patron."

She sat staring at the shot when a shadow fell on the bar and someone filled the seat next to her.

"What's the matter?" Zurik's rich baritone sent a shiver down her spine and tingles in other places. "Did Shelly get you the wrong drink?"

"No." She paused, unsure if she should say more. "Patron was always my favorite."

"Was?"

"I haven't been out drinking in a long time." She laughed as if it was no big deal. "I haven't had the time. This town is crazy."

"It can get pretty rowdy," he admitted as the waitress emerged from the back room with a sub and placed it in front of him. He gave a wink before shoving it in his mouth but Morgan hardly noticed. She yearned for the sting of Patron.

She looked at Zurik who was still watching her as he chewed. Just when she was about to throw it back, Zurik snatched it from her and downed it. She met his electric blue gaze once again. His smile was all too knowing. She looked away from him.

"Patron is like a hot brunette; you can't leave it alone for more than a few minutes, or someone will steal it." His mischievous grin was not lost on her. "Do you want me to order you another?"

"I don't think so," she said.

A knock out brunette in six-inch heels approached Zurik from behind sliding her hands around his waist and whispering in his ear.

"I need to get going," Morgan said excusing herself.

She'd reached the parking lot before someone pulled her to a stop.

"Zurik isn't what you think," Shelly said as Morgan looked back at her.

"Excuse me?" Morgan asked.

"He's a hero," she said louder. "You don't need to protect us from him."

Morgan frowned and looked towards the door Zurik was just heading out tossing his car keys in the air and catching them as he approached the Camaro.

"Who are you Zurik D'Vordi, and what have you done?"

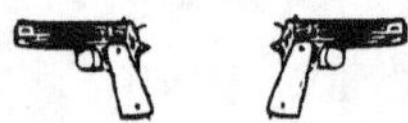

By 11:00 PM, Zurik was making his second trip around campus looking for the creep Jocelyn had told him about in the bar. The damp summer air was almost suffocating. It was a normal North Carolina August, but it would cool off once fall engulfed the state. All was quiet except for the lovebirds he accidentally scared out of the bushes. He pulled out his cell phone and held down the 2 key; it dialed Trent.

"Hey," Trent said after the second ring. "Did you find anything? Are you going home?"

"No," Zurik said. "Just Billy Kingston and Jackey Carson in the bushes."

"Wait," Trent laughed. "They were ...?"

"Trying to get busy. I stepped on her hair."

"Sucks to be Billy," Trent said. Normally Zurik would feel bad for cockblocking a fellow man, but Billy was a shit head, and Zurik couldn't find it within himself to care.

"She was so embarrassed she insisted I walk her home." Zurik frowned. "That's a little weird right? Shouldn't the person you're trying to have sex with be the one you want to walk you home?"

"Maybe." Trent's tone was thoughtful. "Maybe she changed her mind about it and didn't want him to try anything else."

"But I'm Random Stranger Dude," Zurik replied, still feeling puzzled and re-evaluating Billy.

"You have a rep on campus, Zurik. Women know they can go to you for help," Trent said. "In fact, a lot of them come to me for help. Like, a lot."

"That's kind of cool." Zurik's chest swelled with pride and he felt a smile appear on his face.

"Yeah, Zurik. It is."

"Is the old fart still there?" Zurik asked.

"Yep, right next to me, can hear every word."

"Alright, well, I'm going to head back to Cherry Land and make some money."

"You know you have a trust fund right?" Trent asked.

"Yeah, but I didn't earn it," Zurik said.

"So hustling pool is better than taking money that is yours out of a trust?"

"Now we understand each other."

Zurik stood in front of the mansion staring up at the gargoyles perched on the ledge above the door.

Trent followed his gaze as he approached. "What?"

"That one moved," Zurik said pointing out the one to the far left. "I'm sure of it."

"Dude, they're just gargoyles, made of stone, shipped in from Italy."

"I disagree," Zurik said reluctantly following his brother to the front door. The door opened and Rosita smiled at them as they entered. She was a small round woman with a motherly demeanor and the kindest most sincere brown eyes Zurik knew in this world.

"How are you, Boys?" She said in her thick Spanish accent, pulling them each into a tight hug and examining them. "You aren't eating enough I can tell. You go call your mom and I'll whip up something for breakfast."

"Rosita, we're fine you don't need to go to the trouble," Zurik said.

"Nonsense!" she waved their concern away. "I haven't seen you in ages, I won't be able to forgive myself you leave here without full bellies."

She was off before they could protest further. Zurik loved Rosita, but the longer he was here the better the chance he'd run into Markus.

"Come on," Trent said heading up the large curved staircase.

With a resilient huff, he followed. He still didn't understand why Guntar couldn't make a connection to their phones so they could talk to their parents without coming here. He always claimed it was because they were mobile and it would break the magical connection on a regular basis but Zurik was pretty sure that was bullshit. The dude was the most powerful wizard in either dimension. If anyone could figure it out he could. Although doors seemed to give him trouble, so maybe Zurik was giving him too much credit.

As he reached the top of the stairs he heard the computer powering up. As much as he missed his mother, this pseudo connection was almost worse than not seeing her at all. To see her and still be so separate was agony.

Trent sat in front of the screen, another chair pulled up next to him as he fiddled with the camera to make sure they would both be in view. Zurik gave a heavy sigh as he plopped into the chair. Trent pulled up the connection and they waited for an answer. The screen blinked and flickered and then there she was. The most beautiful woman he'd ever seen. Their mother's long blond hair was tousled and unkempt and her eyes were puffy with sleep. Her smile was contagious even as tears filled her eyes.

"My baby boys," she said her voice cracking.

"Hey mom," Trent smiled back the same love mirrored in his eyes.

"Hey," Zurik added looking away from the screen. He could feel his heart breaking with every beat. The tightness in his chest unbearable.

"Where have you been?" she asked. "I've been calling, but your grandfather said you guys haven't been around. If everything OK?"

"It's fine we've just been busy. School has been crazy and Zurik's hunting a fey family before they go underground for the next sixteen years."

"I can't believe how you've grown." She said shaking her head. "My warrior sons. Zurik you'd have fit right in here with your father. He's off dealing with some new threat to the kingdom as we speak."

"How's Faythe?" Trent asked and Zurik looked back to the screen at the mention of their little sister.

"She's doing well. Her coming out ball is fast approaching. Wrath is fighting it with all his limited power in these matters."

"Why?" Trent asked. "The ball is an important right of passage for her."

"Because he's in love with her and won't admit it to himself."

"What?" Zurik saw red at the idea of anyone seeing his baby sister that way.

"Don't worry Zurik, he doesn't even know yet. He watched her grow up. He'll hate every suitor for a while and then I'll tell him why he hates them and then he'll panic and they'll date and it will either work or it won't."

"How can you be so calm?" Zurik asked.

"I love Wrath and after having you ripped from my arms, I'm just happy to be a part of Faythe's life." She gave a weak smile. "Are there any special ladies in your lives I should know about?"

"School is kind of all-consuming," Trent said but there was a note of sadness in his tone that permeated the room.

"And you Zurik?"

"No one special," he gave a half smile that didn't come close to his eyes. He had to get out of here. "I have to go, there are fey running around kidnapping people."

"But you just got here?" Marina's voice was so sad, he couldn't look at the screen.

"Love you, Mom, tell Dad I said hi," he walked out of the room as Trent apologized for his behavior. Seeing her and not being able to hug her or hold her hand when she was so clearly heartbroken was just too much. Zurik blinked back the tears that threatened to fall and headed for the door.

"Zurik? Are you done already?" Rosita called after him as he reached the door.

"I need to go, Rosita, it was nice seeing you." With that, he left the house and walked down the long driveway toward town.

# FOUR
# LONGING AND COLD COFFEE

Morgan sat in the liquor store parking lot. Coffee in hand as she fought with herself. She didn't need alcohol. But she wanted it. As long as she didn't need it she'd be OK. One bottle wouldn't hurt. Especially if she got the little bottle. Just a nip.

*No, that's how people end up in a barrel. It always starts with a nip.*

She looked at Cavazos' coffee getting cold in the center console and started the car. She pulled out of the lot and headed to the station. When she entered she found Cavazos' chair empty. A fellow detective sat at the adjacent desk.

"Where's Paul?" she asked the rookie. He gave her the cocky smile she'd become used to in this hick town.

"Can't you even find your own partner?"

She smiled back and fluttered her eyelashes. "Oh silly me! I forgot I'm not in New York anymore! It's sad to think New Yorkers are more polite."

"Morgan." Reynolds barked her name. "In here, please."

The rookie's face went pale as she entered the captain's office. Like she'd tattle on him or something. She glared at him and resisted the urge stick out her tongue. At least if they got to know her they could find actual shortcomings to pick on and give up this blanket insult crap.

"Here's your coffee, Cavazos," she said as she handed him the now lukewarm beverage. He sipped it and smiled. Whatever they'd been talking about before her arrival must be bad for him not to even complain even a little about his less than hot coffee.

"What's going on?"

"We think the FBI are the ones who tampered with the tape."

"What?" She sat down in the brown squishy chair across from the captain's desk.

"It was expertly done, but we have one bit of footage and we can't see his face but remember that suit that was here a few weeks ago advising on a possible serial killer?"

"Yeah, Agent—some kind of bird?" she asked looking to Cavazos for backup but he only shrugged.

"Agent Hawk," Reynolds said.

"Yeah, he had me fetch him random unsolved cases. Missing persons, murders, but there was no connection that I could see." She paused. "Accept Zurik. He was involved in three of them. That's why I recognized him on the tape from the video store."

Cavazos and Reynolds exchanged a look like they were making a connection but she was still missing pieces. "You don't think he's a serial killer do you?"

"Don't you?" Cavazos said. "He took down those guys in the alley like they were nothing."

"I've been going over it and over it, don't you think those guys were—ya know—hunting the girls in the beginning? I mean they have some pretty standard 'pack hunting' characteristics."

"What are you saying?"

"I think Zurik is a vigilante." Saying it out loud sounded crazier than in her head but the evidence was all there. A bit circumstantial but present and accounted for. "Think about it, he has the means to work on cases as often as he wants. People trust him in this town. The bartender just last night told me he's a hero."

"You're saying," Cavazos paused as if the connection were difficult for him to make. "He's Batman."

She nodded. "The concept is the same, yes."

"How much time does the FBI typically spend on vigilantes?" Cavazos asked. "That part wasn't in the comics."

Morgan glared.

Cavazos chuckled to himself. "Wait, bartender?"

"I don't know. But more importantly, why would they help a vigilante?" Reynolds asked interrupting Cavazos' realization. They'd have to discuss it sooner or later. Cavazos was one of the only people here who knew about her drinking problem.

"Because Hawk is on Mr. D'Vordi's payroll as well as the FBI's." She said drawing their attention back to the case at hand.

"I want you two to go see if there's a copy of the tape in the video store. All our copies are junk or tampered with." Reynolds ordered. "Maybe if we get more evidence our mole will show himself again to save D'Vordi and we can kill two birds with one stone."

They nodded and headed out into the bullpen. She grabbed her blazer and hit the rookie in the back of the head with a file before they headed out into the parking lot.

"You went to a bar by yourself?" Cavazos snapped as they got in her work car. A nondescript beige sedan. "And where did you buy this coffee? Antarctica?"

"I was fine," she lied. She'd have to wait to tell him about Zurik saving her from herself until it was absolutely necessary or he'd never leave her alone again. "And I was stuck in traffic. That damn train goes slower every morning I swear."

"It's only been a couple years Morgan, you're still new to this." A veteran AA member, Cavazos was right but she couldn't think about that right now. Her sponsor would be proud. "And I told you to avoid the train tracks."

Morgan smiled. It was a little sad how easy it was to deceive Cavazos. He hated the train. He'd be raving about it for the next hour or so and he'd make sure to point out all the ways over and under it.

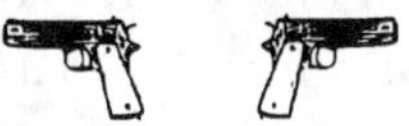

Zurik reached the four-mile marker as the familiar roar of Trent's Jeep Wrangler sounded behind him. He uncrossed his arms and kept walking. He knew he couldn't get away, but he didn't want his brother to see how much their mother affected him.

It took Trent another few minutes to catch up. He pulled off the road in front of Zurik and turned in the driver's seat to glare at his older brother. He hopped out of the car and crossed his arms as Zurik approached.

"What the hell, Dude?" Trent asked anger burned in his eyes.

"You know I don't like seeing her like that." Zurik snapped. He knew he was being an ass, but seeing her on the other side of the screen was worse than not seeing her. Why couldn't anyone understand that?

"She needs to see us, you don't think this is hard on her too? That seeing us grow up without her is easy? You can see the hurt in her eyes as she asks us about mundane shit."

"Yeah and there's nothing we can do about it," Zurik was yelling now. Anything to avoid the pain his mother's absence brought.

"Yes you can, you can sit your ass in the chair, look her in the eye and answer her questions. You can pretend you care about someone other than yourself for five minutes!"

Zurik saw red. Before he could stop himself, he threw a left hook right into Trent's jaw. His brother fell to the ground holding his face. He glared up at Zurik. And Zurik saw in his eyes the very moment he switched from being Trent D'Vordi, a lawyer in training and all around good guy, to just being a little pain in the ass brother.

Trent launched himself at Zurik, using his larger size to knock Zurik to the ground. Zurik put his arms up to block the series of blows that Trent rained down on him until he snapped too. Shoving his brother back a few feet he leaped onto him and punched him in the face until Trent got a hold of Zurik's jacket and rolled into the ditch.

Neither one noticed as a black Mercedes pulled up behind the Jeep. Markus stepped out and watched the scuffle unfolding in the ditch. Growing more and more impatient until he stepped in.

Markus grabbed each brother by the back of the neck and pulled them apart like two warring puppies and tossed them in opposite directions.

"Enough!" His voice boomed through the trees and several birds flew off into the sky to escape the perceived danger while the rest of the forest went silent. "What is going on here? Rosita called and said Trent left the house in a rage? Zurik you walked out on your mother's call?"

"Yeah I did," Zurik said as he stood. "And I'm not calling her again."

He stalked off toward town again while Trent dusted himself off.

"I expect this kind of petty bullshit from him but you, Trent?"

"You should have seen her face, Grandpa," Trent said. "She was heartbroken and he couldn't care less."

"Did it ever occur to you that he cares too much?" Markus asked. "I tried to raise you boys right, to not be afraid of your emotions. To let you grieve in your own way at the loss of your home. Your family. But Zurik never did. He never cried, never acted out until Selena died. And even then, he has never grieved her either. I hoped this connection with your home and mother would force him to let it all that out. I guess I was wrong. He seems more withdrawn than ever."

Zurik slid the tequila back and held it in his mouth for a moment. Closing his eyes he allowed the liquor to burn his throat a bit before sending it to his stomach. He took a deep breath and leaned his head back. The booth dipped and a dainty feminine hand touched his knee.

"Jo, you have perfect timing," he said opening his eyes. Jocelyn was a tall brunette with dark skin and legs that went on for days. Legs he could lose himself in. They'd met in this very bar almost a year ago and she'd been the only woman who didn't bug him about being in a real relationship. "I've had a hell of a day, let's grab a pizza and head to your place."

He slid her hand up his thigh to the erection burning against his jeans. She smiled and pulled back.

"Not tonight my friend."

He frowned. "Really?" usually she was down whenever. She'd even helped him on a stake-out last week.

"I know you, Zurik. You're feeling bad right now. Maybe the bad guy got away or you got in a fight with your grandfather or maybe Trent called you out on your bullshit—"

"He punched me."

"What?"

"I punched him first."

She glared. "So you're looking to slip into someone else's sheets for a night and forget your troubles. And normally, I'd be that woman for you. But after everything we've been through Z, it's only a matter of time before one of us catches feelings and I can't go there with you."

He frowned again. Why was sex always connected to feelings for chicks? And why couldn't she have feelings for him? "Why can't you have feelings for me?"

"Because what we do is too important. I can't risk it. Now that I know, what I know." She looked toward the bar, shaking her head. "I've done the whole, love a guy who can't love you back thing. And I don't want that with you."

"I'm not some super asshole. I can love back." He paused. Could he though?

"I know honey," she rubbed his leg again her words slow, clear, and reassuring.

"What has Trent told you about me?" Zurik would kill that little shit. He was like an open book about everything.

"He told me about your girlfriend. From high school, Selena."

Zurik looked away. No one said her name around him. Ever. He visited her grave sometimes but only in the middle of the night. When no one was around. And usually with a bottle of Jack to share.

"I know you don't like to talk about it and I won't force you, but if you want to be in a relationship with someone new, you'll need to deal with that."

"How?" he snapped. "How do you just deal with someone dying because of you? Please enlighten me so I can 'get over it'."

"Don't pull that angry shit with me," Jo's voice was quiet but somehow angrier than his. "You wanna push people away and be sad the rest of your life, that's your choice but you will not take your shit out on me."

He looked into his beer. "Sorry."

"Also, do you know the brunette at the bar is following you?" She sounded perfectly normal now. How did she do that?

He leaned into the tale to see who she was talking about. Morgan looked back at her club soda at the bar. "Yeah, she's the Dick that's trying to lock me up."

"Oh," Jo eyed Morgan for a moment. "Let's go back to my place."

She stood up and waited for him to scoot to the edge of the booth. She stepped between his legs, her breasts right at his head level. She tipped his chin up so his eyes met hers. "No sex."

"No sex," he agreed. Even if it wasn't the evening he'd planned, at least he wouldn't have to be alone.

# FIVE
# MISSING

Morgan watched as the knockout dragged Zurik away. No doubt for a night of passion. On the plus side, he'd probably be too preoccupied to kill anyone tonight. On the downside, she didn't envy that girl hearing the news of his arrest in the next few days. The news coverage would go on and on about this one. They'd give him an awful nickname that Turner would argue prejudiced the jury.

Morgan turned back to her club soda. Maybe Cavazos would bring her a coffee once they got wherever the two lovebirds were off too. She put a few dollars on the bar and slid off her stool to follow Zurik.

"You forget what I said?" The bartender called after her.

"Nope, but I still have to do my job," Morgan said with a sympathetic shrug.

"Talk to the female students on campus. The ones who've been there a while. Talk to the woman who frequents this bar. Talk to anyone who actually knows him. With the acceptation of that guy." She indicated a football player by the jukebox. "That guy got rough with his date a few weeks back and Zurik straightened him out. I'm no lawyer but probably not by the letter of the law."

Morgan eyed the man in the letterman jacket. He was good-looking, clean shaven. The woman he was with now didn't appear uncomfortable or worried. Her curly blonde hair was nearly down to her waist and bobbed around her head as she swayed to the music.

"His date seems happy now," Morgan said looking back to Shelly. The bartender shook her head. Morgan slid off her stool and headed over to the group. She held up her badge. "Detective Jennifer Morgan, can I ask you a few questions about Zurik D'Vordi?"

The jock nodded and stepped off the dance floor.

"Shelly said you two had an altercation? Can I get your name?"

"Billy Kingston," he sounded nervous. "I don't wanna press charges or anything."

"What happened with Zurik?" the blonde chimed in.

"Do you know him?" Morgan asked.

"Not personally but word is he's someone you can count on if you feel unsafe at a party or anything else. It's practically in the handbook."

"And it doesn't weird you guys out that a nearly 30-year-old man is at campus parties?" Morgan asked.

"His brother, Trent, goes to SU, so not really. He also stands in for the band when Brandon is too drunk or high to sing." She added.

"Billy, can you tell me what happened to you?" Morgan persisted.

"I got into an argument with my date and before I knew it he was wailing on me."

"An argument?" Morgan asked. "Nothing physical? You didn't hit her or anything?"

He looked at his date and shook his head. "No nothing like that."

Morgan made a mental note that he probably had. "Can I have her name? To ask her about the incident?"

"She's gone, she doesn't go to this school she was just visiting for the weekend. She's back in Greensboro."

"Just the same, I'd like to speak with her."

"I don't have her number but I can ask around."

"You do that," Morgan said more certain than ever that the jock had done something wrong.

Jocelyn slid from the bed with a stretch. Her arms over her head, she glanced out the open window. The sun spilled in through her white curtains, illuminating the small dorm room. She looked over her shoulder at Zurik. Half naked and asleep in her bed. Part of her was sad at the loss of his physical touch. He was a fantastic lover. But she could feel herself falling for him and knew going down that road would only end in pain and misery.

She put on her pants and a light jacket and headed out to the coffee cart. One of the bonuses of living in Stephenson Hall was the proximity to the best coffee cart on campus. A line had already formed so she took her place at the back and looked out over the road. It was the main road in and out of campus with a speed limit of 15 and large grassy areas on either side. Jo was watching a car she didn't recognize, a big grey van with no windows and a rusted bumper when someone tapped her on the shoulder. She turned to see Missy Halloway.

"Hey, Missy, what's up?"

"I saw you with Zurik last night and I was wondering if you two were official yet?"

"Oh no, we're just friends." Jo laughed trying not to let her heart hurt. It was her decision and he'd been respectful and amazing as always.

"Really?" Missy looked shocked. "Well, shit I guess I lost that bet."

"Bet?" Jo asked anger rising up in her chest.

"Yeah, I bet Vanessa five bucks you'd bag the oldest D'Vordi."

"Are you serious?"

"I never joke about money," Missy winked. "I really am surprised though. You guys seemed really close at the club last week."

"We were but it was a fling type thing. Nothing to write home about."

"You think his little brother would be interested in me?" Missy asked. Trent's tastes were not Jo's area of expertise.

"I really wouldn't know. I've never seen him with or heard him talk about a girl."

"You think he's gay?" Missy asked. The fear in her eyes at the possibility was enough to bring a smile to Jo's lips.

"I don't think so, but I really wouldn't know Missy--you should just ask him out and see how it goes."

"I guess so." Missy patted her pockets. "Oh crap, I forgot my wallet in my room. I'll be right back."

Missy ran off across the street and Jo moved forward in line. She would have bought Missy's coffee if she'd given her half a second to offer.

Jocelyn ordered two coffees one with a splash of milk and her usual caramel macchiato. As she turned from the cart she saw Miss running back across the road. The grey van flew around the corner and hit her. Jocelyn felt the coffee cups slip from her hands as her throat began to burn. The screams cutting the air shook her to her core. The driver got out of the car and grabbed Missy's limp body. Jocelyn was halfway to her when they tossed her in the back of the van. Jo screamed at them and pain ripped through her throat. The men smirked as they shut the door and drove off towards the main road.

She turned around to see Zurik running after it wearing nothing but an unbuttoned pair of jeans. The barista from the coffee cart placed a hand on her shoulder and Jocelyn turned to see her out of breath with her phone pressed to her ear.

"Yes, I need to report a kidnapping," she said as she struggled to catch her breath.

Morgan held a coffee in her hand and didn't bother removing her aviator sunglasses as she approached the officers already on the scene.

"What's the deal?" Morgan asked Cavazos as she approached. Sipping the coffee and gritting her teeth at the burned beans and charred aftertaste. She missed Dunk's.

"A group of students saw the abduction. It was a large van and multiple male perps. The van matches the description of the one used in three other abductions in the last three months. And you're never gonna guess who one of the witnesses was."

She pulled the glasses off her face, not caring who saw the bags under her eyes, as she turned to look at the group of students. Sure enough, Zurik D'Vordi stood in the middle of them with one arm around the brunette he'd left the bar with last night. He was barefoot and shirtless. Like he'd rushed out of bed when the incident occurred. She felt a pang of something strange in her chest at the sight of him with his arm around the brunette. She couldn't place it. Fear? Regret? Anger? No. It didn't fit any of those. But it wasn't pleasant.

She walked up with her eyes wide. "Well, well, well, Mr. D'Vordi. I get a call to leave you alone and you fall right back onto my radar. What do you suppose that's about?"

"Just lucky I guess." He smiled. "You know you missed me."

"Zurik, Missy was abducted and it's my fault. Leave your shit at home for this one," the brunette snapped.

"Sorry Jo," he gave her a guilty smile and pulled her in for a hug. She pulled back and walked towards the officer who was ready to take her statement.

"What happened?"

"Nothing we're just friends," Zurik said putting his hands in his pockets.

Morgan gave an exasperated sigh even as she felt the tension in her chest recede. "I meant with Missy."

"Oh," his cheeks flushed slightly. "Sorry, Jo went down to the coffee cart, and her friend Missy was in line. I guess she forgot her wallet and ran back to get it. That's when the van hit her. I heard the sound, looked out the window and ran outside. By the time we reached the road the van was gone."

"Who's 'we'?" Morgan asked taking notes on a small notepad.

"The Barista, Jo, and myself."

"You were the only three to try and stop it?"

"Yeah. I think everyone was in shock. It's not every day you see someone get run over and thrown in the back of a van."

"Tell me what's actually going on," Morgan said. "I've been researching you since I was assigned the video store murders. Your name came up in the other missing women cases. Why were you at each one?"

"You wouldn't believe me if I told you."

"Try me."

"I'm a PI."

"Try again. You're not licensed."

"I'm studying. Haven't passed the test yet."

She narrowed her eyes. "You look like your telling the truth but there's a smell to you. The very distinct smell of bullshit."

He gave a half laugh. "Believe me or not. It's up to you."

"Is this connected to the video store incident? We never found the bodies but those guys were stalking the young women at the beginning of the tape, weren't they. You're some kind of vigilante."

"I'm just someone who's trying to do their best," he answered.

"You need to do better, Zurik, or you'll end up in jail."

"Are you threatening me?" he asked, narrowing his eyes on her.

"Do you need to be threatened?"

"I didn't want things to go like this. You're a good cop and this town needs good cops but you need to get off my back and let me do my job."

"What is your job, Mr. D'Vordi?" she snapped. Her voice getting louder and louder as she went. Her anger was completely uncontrollable. "Killing kidnappers? Killing the bad people in this world? You can't do that! You hand them over to us and we make sure they pay for their crimes! That's how this works."

Zurik leaned in and adrenaline shot through her body. "You aren't equipped to deal with the things I do. Now back off or I'll make you back off."

"I'd love to see you try." No sooner had the words come out of her mouth than the angry bark of Captain Reynolds broke the silence around them.

"Morgan," he said again. "Now."

She held Zurik's eerie blue gaze for a moment longer before returning to where the captain stood. He glared at her.

"Screaming at a witness to a crime, in front of the other witnesses?" he hissed from between clenched teeth. "What has gotten into you?"

"He knows more than he's telling," she snapped.

"That's not how you get information."

"Great, I'd love to hear from you about your expertise in the area. I mean it's not like my close rate in New York was better than your entire squad's combined or anything."

Reynolds straightened and closed his eyes. He took a deep breath before looking at her again. "Walk away." She opened her mouth to protest. "No, Morgan. You're suspended. You either figure out how to take orders or you will be fired. The FBI said he's off limits. That's the end of it. Now go home and cool off. I don't want to see you until Monday."

Morgan's breathing was rapid as she returned to her car. She slammed it into reverse and peeled out of the parking lot. Unable to control her rage she drove until she saw the neon sign for the local bar Cherry Land.

# SIX

# LET'S GO FOR A RIDE

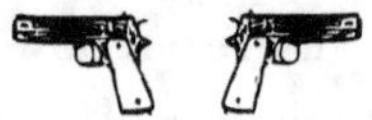

Morgan cradled her 9mm Glock in her hands. Elbows slightly bent, leaning into the weapon as she aimed. The plastic safety glasses slid down her nose providing the perfect distraction to try and shoot through. The ancient AC in the range did little to cool the oppressive North Carolina summer heat.

She squeezed the trigger, slowly at first. The gun rocked back and the bullet flew at her target. As it moved back into place she squeezed again and again until the clip was empty. She locked the slider into condition two and placed it on the stainless steel shelf in front of her as she flipped the switch and the tiny motor squealed to life, bringing the target closer. She looked at her grouping. Not her best shooting.

This case had her shook. It was affecting everything in her life. Her shooting, her sobriety, her relations with her partner. She barely held onto her sanity yesterday. She sat in the bar parking lot for over an hour.

She knew she should just back off. The FBI could handle D'Vordi. But there was something there.

Something about him that screamed at her. She had to know what it was.

The door creaked, announcing the arrival of another officer.

"So, are you really going to take this suspension lying down?" Cavazos' drawl tugged at her heartstrings.

"If I don't, I may fall off the wagon." The words came out like a joke but she knew Cavazos would see right through it.

"How close were you?" he stood up, crossing his well muscled arms over his plump belly. All business.

"You know, teetering on the edge, watching the ground fly by, contemplating just—" she made a jumping gesture.

"How long have you been feeling like this?"

"Since the FBI kicked us off the case," she admitted.

"Forget D'Vordi. There's a few murder cases that look suspicious. Reynolds wants you to focus on those when you get back."

He left her in the range. Feeling as if his duty was done. The words 'Forget D'Vordi' rang in her ears. By the time she got to her car, it was all she could focus on. She pulled open the glove box and the nip of Fire Ball fell out. The small plastic bottle hit her hand and landed on the floor with a thud. She grabbed it. Holding the cool plastic in her hand. She gripped the red cap and twisted until the snap of the seal breaking filled her car. She looked around the parking lot. She shook her head. This was ridiculous. As she moved to twist the cap back on the burning cinnamon smell singed her nose and pushed her right off the wagon.

The white ball rolled over the green felt just fast enough to knock the last striped ball into the corner pocket and hover at the edge.

"That's what, $500?" Zurik asked the trucker.

The man pulled out his wallet with a murderous glare.

"Double or nothing? What do you say?"

The man slapped the money on the table.

"Say no," the female voice was familiar but there was something off about her words so Zurik couldn't quite place it. He turned to see Morgan approaching with two shots in her hands and a beer bottle tucked under her arm. She wore a red v-neck t-shirt and tight blue jeans. The outfit accentuated her curves in a way her pantsuit never could.

"What the hell happened to you?" he asked eyeing the shots and beer.

"You did. God, you're so dumb for a hot guy. Your looks got you through life, didn't they. You were totally content with that."

"No." He scoffed. She was a mean drunk.

"That's right you have grandpa's money to get you through life. Pays for your big-time lawyer and gets you out of all kinds of scrapes."

"I make my own money," Zurik said. "You really judgey for a white girl from New York."

"What's that supposed to mean? You think you're some kind of Mr. Darcy and I'm what?"

"Kitty."

"Ouch," she leaned back and screwed her face up as if he'd actually hurt her. "That was uncalled for."

"Sorry," he said as the trucker walked away. "I was embarrassed."

"How do you even know that reference?"

"My first girlfriend was a huge Jane Austen fan, we used to read the books at the same time and talk about them."

Morgan stared at him like he was some strange creature from an alien planet. "What? You read the books?"

"Yeah and watched the show and the movie with Kira Knightley. I would have done anything for that girl."

"What happened to her?" Morgan handed him one of her shots.

He threw it back. "She died."

Morgan frowned, he could see her spidey sense tingling. "You're either a serial killer or the most unlucky bastard in the history of the earth."

"I'm not psychotic." He snapped picking up his beer and taking a drink. She was really hard to talk to.

"Most serial killers are psychopaths actually," she said as threw back her shot. "Psychotics are actually your standard definition of crazy. Psychopaths are just like anyone else. But they don't feel compassion or empathy for other people. But they mimic it so you might not even notice."

"I'm not that either."

She pursed her lips. "Fine, let's play pool."

"One game then I gotta go."

"Where?"

"I have to go shopping."

She frowned again. "Someone's birthday?"

"Not exactly."

"Mind if I tag along?"

She probably just wanted to tail him, but he could use the company.

Morgan stood in line at the pickup counter as Zurik paid for the sandwiches and they brought out bags filled with bottled water. The House of Pie was within walking distance from the bar and she'd made it relatively unscathed. One stop sign would forever have a piece of her though. Literally, she'd run into it and somehow gotten her hair caught.

"How much food do you need?" Morgan asked as Zurik approached her, tucking his wallet into his back pocket. Her eyes lingering on his well-formed rear end.

"They're not for me," he said grabbing the bags.

Morgan frowned but he didn't explain. The haze of alcohol was still too thick for her to focus. She grabbed a couple of bags and headed after him to his car.

"Where are we going? I can't get in there with you."

"Then put the bags in the passenger seat and I'll see you later." He said opening the door for her put down the food and drinks. "But you shouldn't drive. Want me to call you a cab?"

She looked back at Cherry Land. "Hold on."

Morgan placed the bags on the seat and pulled her phone out of her back pocket and texted Cavazos.

*Getting in Zurich s car*
*If I never calm bak arrest hm*

"Okay," she said with a laugh. "If you kill me, Paul will find you."

"Who's Paul?"

"Never mind," she waved her hand at him. Better if she didn't reveal her master plan to the criminal. She pushed the bags aside and hopped into the car.

He laughed as he got in and started the engine. He drove down the main drag and turned away from the college toward the edge of town and the National Forest. The back roads were winding and dark and her fear grew as they approached the river. Her heart began to race as he cut the engine. She pulled up Google Maps and dropped a pin to alert Cavazos of her location.

Zurik got out and leaned back in to grab the food. He looked at her still buckled seat belt and paused. "You coming?"

"I know I was joking about you killing me, but—you aren't really going to murder me are you?"

"Not tonight," he stood and shut the door, walking away from the car. She leaned forward to look out his window and watch him as he approached a dim orange glow at the edge of the riverbank.

She frowned as people came forward and Zurik gave each a sandwich and bottle of water. Feeling like a jerk she jumped out of the car and made her way to the bank. All she could focus on was putting one foot in front of the other on the uneven ground. Every step she didn't fall on her face felt like a victory.

"You hustled that trucker out of his hard-earned money to buy a meal for the homeless?" she asked unsure of the morality here.

"I hustled an abusive prick out of his money so I could buy food for the homeless." Zurik corrected.

The man who was waiting for a sandwich laughed. "Do you only feed us with stolen money?"

Zurik smiled. "No, I just feel bad keeping money I earned by less than reputable means."

"I don't care where it comes from friend, as long as it ends up in my belly." The man walked back toward the fire in the trashcan nearby as Zurik handed out the rest of the sandwiches.

Morgan felt her mind starting to clear as they walked back to the car. "Who are you?"

"I'm a playboy with too much time on his hands and a quick temper."

"No really?" Morgan asked. Her frown deepening as she thought about what she knew of Zurik. "How many times have you done this?"

"Once a week."

She looked at him until he gave a shrug and continued. "I'm a guy who likes to help people."

"Why?"

"Why does anyone do anything?" he asked. Just as she was about to protest his deflection his phone rang out with *Bad Boys* by Inner Circle. He opened it and smiled as he turned on the charm. "Twitch, my favorite lady friend, what do you have for me? OK, text me the location. Yep, I'll check it out tonight." He paused as he listened to the person on the other end of the call and looked at Morgan. "I just have to drop Detective Morgan off…. She what?"

He put a hand over the receiver of the phone. "You got suspended?"

"Turns out yelling at you was my last misstep. I'm out till next week."

"Huh."

"What do you expect?" she scoffed. "Your guy at the FBI was very persistent."

"My guy?" his eyes grew. "The FBI?"

Shit. She'd convinced herself he was behind the call. Apparently, she was wrong.

"What FBI guy?"

"I can't talk about it." She said honestly. "I shouldn't be here."

"I'll drop you off. Twitch?" he said into the phone. "Can you check out this FBI connection?… Yeah, thanks."

He hung up the phone.

"Where are you going? Who were you talking too?"

"I can't talk about it." He said using her words. She glared.

"Really? Can you lose your job for talking?"

"Worse," he said honestly. "You could lose your life."

# SEVEN
# Monsters?

Zurik parked down the road from the address Twitch gave him. He slipped into the shadows of the trees and crept toward the dim glow of a manmade structure. As he got closer her could see a large farmhouse with several other buildings close by. A few lights were on inside the farmhouse and there was a light off the back of the house illuminating a path to an old barn.

Moving on the balls of his feet, he approached the side of the house and peered into the window. Through the curtains, he could only make out a small group of men playing cards at the table. Squinting he searched their features for the telltale signs they weren't quite human. He'd need to get closer but first, he'd scout the out-buildings. If he found the missing women he'd know what he was in for before getting into a fight.

He pulled back from the window as he felt metal on his wrist followed by the distinct clicking of cuffs. He looked down to see Morgan smiling at him with the other cuff attached to her arm.

"You're under arrest Zurik D'Vordi, and not even the FBI can help you this time."

"Seriously?" he whispered. "Go home and sleep it off, we can do this tomorrow."

"You have the right to remain silent. Anything you say can and will be used against you in a court of law."

"Shhh!" He hissed glaring at her. "What am I being arrested for? Was there a private property sign I missed?"

"The van used to kidnap Missy is under that tarp," she pointed over her shoulder to the driveway.

"Again I ask why I'm being arrested?"

"You have to be in on it, how else would you know how to find this place?"

"I know a computer wiz who likes to hack government facilities for the challenge. She hacked the DMV and gave me the address. You were there when I got the call, remember?"

"You really are a vigilante!" she said her eyes went wide.

"You caught me, now go back to the police station and get back up."

"I can't," she held up her hand pulling his along with it. "I left the key in my car."

"You drove?"

"No I Uber'd I've never done it before but the lady was super nice. She drives drunk kids home all the time—"

The sound of a screen door squealing open and slamming shut rattled the night air. He put his finger on his lips to silence her and leaned against the wall.

"I heard something," a deep voice slid through the darkness to their location.

"You need to get out of here now," Zurik whispered.

"And you what? Need to chat about proper lawn maintenance?"

"Morgan," he stressed her name like he was speaking to a child. Knowing it was futile, a child would have listened by now.

"Over here," the deep voice was accompanied by footsteps. Lots of footsteps.

"Things are about to get ugly," Zurik said through gritted teeth. "They aren't human, you're gun won't work." He placed his hand over the shackle on her wrist and yanked. The metal held fast. "What the—"

He looked to the corner of the house where a light was moving closer and pulled again. He should be able to break these cuffs without an issue. He pulled Morgan into the light to inspect the metal. He cursed as the small markings on the cuff glinted in the moonlight.

"What the hell is this?" he asked looking back to the corner of the house. He was about to have to fight the fey while attached to a drunk detective.

"They were my dad's," she said pulling her gun as the group came around the corner. The older ones looked almost human, but the young had cat-like eyes and elongated canines. Their skin looked like the scars of 3rd-degree burns

"I wondered when you'd show up D'Vordi," Dominick was one Zurik had fought many times. He was old even when Zurik first met him. Of course, Zurik was only twelve at the time. And Lex had done most of the fighting. But even now, Dominick was still only second in command. The group was small. Seven in total. Zurik smiled. If he'd depleted their ranks this much he was doing a damn good job this time.

"Where's your dad, Dominick?" Zurik asked. Playing it cool as he tried to push Morgan behind him.

"Looks like you brought us a gift," The fey said as he licked his lips revealing a set of elongated canines. "She looks perfect. Older than we usually go for, but I don't mind. My last bride was so young, she never fought me. Not once. It was incredibly disappointing."

"I'm not here to please you," Morgan said raising her weapon. "I'm here to arrest you. SPD, everybody get down on the ground now!"

No one moved.

"Morgan," Zurik said, his exasperated sigh enunciating her name. "They aren't people."

"What?"

The first fey attacked and Zurik blocked his punch and moved to deliver his own but was stopped by the cuffs and Morgan. The fey delivered a blow to Zurik's gut and he doubled over as nausea consumed him and he fought to get air back in his lungs.

"I will shoot!" Morgan yelled from where she stood next to him. The fey hissed and moved to attack her. She fired one shot into his chest. He fell to the ground but he'd be back up in a moment.

"Use my gun," Zurik groaned as he stood, offering her the pistol.

"I'm not using your gun, I shoot with mine all the time, I'm used to it."

"Yours won't work," he snapped before dodging a blow from another attacker. Kicking the fey back he grabbed Morgan's gun by the top so it failed to slide and ripped it from her hands. He tossed it away from them and offered her his pistol again. "They aren't human."

He pointed to the one on the ground she'd shot moments earlier as it rolled to its side and stood up.

Her eyes widened when he pulled the machete off his belt and decapitated the next fey to come his way. The body turned to dust before it hit the ground.

"Holy shit," Morgan whispered.

"You can't fall apart now," Zurik said as he fought. "Those women need our help."

Another fey ran at them. She aimed, Zurik's larger gun bulky and awkward in her hands as she squeezed the trigger. Aiming for center mass. The bullet ripped through the fey's shoulder.

"The heart," Zurik barked.

"I'm working on it, Dickweed," she let the gun settle in her hands and readjusted her stance. She squeezed the trigger again. This time hitting the fey in the abdomen.

"You're over-correcting!" Zurik screamed as he blocked a fey attack. Holding one hand next to her so she could aim. "Did you just call me 'Dickweed'?"

"Thank you Captain Obvious! If you have anything further to add keep it to yourself!"

She squeezed the trigger slowly. The crack of the firing pin filled the hollow as the bullet hit center mass and the fey exploded into fine golden dust.

"You don't handle pressure well, do you?" he snapped after decapitating the fey at his feet.

"I'm a cop," she snapped. "I can handle pressure."

"Really?" he put a hand on his chest. "Because you were lashing out at me. That's not a sign of 'handling' pressure last I checked."

He looked around. Dominick and last two fey were long gone. "Looks like we're going to have to hunt the rest of them down as we look for the girls."

"Women."

He rolled his eyes. "The victims. Where are the keys to these things?"

"We can't go hunting for keys, they could take the women and run."

"What if we slash the tires on the van?"

"Do you have a single law-abiding bone in your body?"

He looked at his chest patted his abdomen. "I can't find one—"

"UGH," she gave an exaggerated gesture. "Let's go, we need to clear the house and—" sirens cut her off. The flashing blue lights danced on the leaves as they approached.

"You actually had backup?"

"I was dropping pins all night. I guess Paul got worried."

# EIGHT
# CELEBRATE

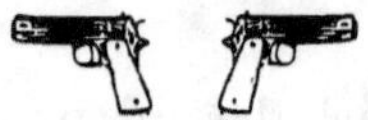

Cavazos' tan cruiser pulled up onto the lawn first and he ran to them. Wrapping his arms around Morgan's shoulders and pulling her in close.

"I thought you were dead!" He snapped as he pulled back to look her over. "You dropped a pin in the river after texting me that Zurik might kill you? What the fuck, Morgan?"

"That was supposed to just be by the river. We fed the homeless people."

"And this?" Cavazos gestured to the house and surrounding area. "What the hell is this?"

"This is where the kidnap victims are being held. Come on let's go find em."

"Morgan," Zurik said pulling her to a stop when he didn't follow. "We need to get out of these cuffs. The perps are long gone by now."

"Why are you handcuffed to our number one suspect who we aren't supposed to be investigating?" Cavazos asked.

"It seemed like a good idea at the time."

"Can we all agree it wasn't a good idea and should never happen again?" Cavazos asked. Zurik and Morgan nodded. EMT's and uniformed officers were gathering around as well as a few of the other detectives. Zurik grabbed her hand in the hopes that no one else gathered would realize they were cuffed. She moved in front of their clasped hands to further the illusion

"The missing women are here somewhere. There are still a few perps lurking around so proceed with caution." Morgan said to everyone gathered.

"Did you catch any of them?" one of the detectives snickered. He was young. Zurik would guess a rookie. Of course, he'd be the one most intimidated by a strong female in the department.

Zurik eyed the twerp. Morgan made a lot of potentially costly mistakes tonight but she'd also killed her first fey. Zurik toyed with the blade between his fingers. Before he could give the detective the scare he deserved Cavazos barked some orders.

"You heard her, move out! Report anything and everything back to me. And call in another bus, we have four missing women and one ambulance, do the math people!"

As the rookie walked past them Zurik tossed the blade into the ground by his feet. It barely sliced the side of the faux leather shoes.

"What the hell?" the rookie yelled stepping back from the knife.

"Sorry man, it just slipped right out of my fingers." Zurik picked up the blade and rotated it in his hands, showing off his skill.

"You better watch it," he snapped.

"I think you should too," Zurik smiled.

"Come on Zurik," Morgan tugged at his cuffed hand. He watched the rookie for a few more seconds before turning his attention to her.

"Why don't you go home, before Captain Reynolds gets here," Cavazos suggested. "I'll tell him what happened, you guys found the victims and all and that I sent you home for the night."

Morgan nodded and headed down the driveway. "Thanks, Cavazos."

"You work with a bunch of assholes," Zurik said as they made their way to the Uber.

"Yep, I do."

"You made her wait?"

"Yes, I did," as soon as they were around the corner where no one could see them she launched herself into the air, pulling him along with her. "That was the most incredible fight of my life!"

Zurik felt a chuckle rumble up in his chest. "It would have been better if four of them hadn't gotten away."

"Yeah but there's no bringing someone in and hoping the jury or judge sees the evidence the way you do. No slimy defense attorneys. No doubt that you have the right guy."

She grabbed him around the neck and laid a kiss on his lips. He stiffened for a moment as the shock of what was happening wore off. He slid his free hand around her waist and pulled her soft curves against him. Growling into her mouth. She tasted even better than he'd imagined.

She pushed him back looking up at him from beneath her lashes.

"I'm sorry—"

"What for?" he asked sliding his hands over her hips.

"You're with that girl aren't you?"

"Jo?" he asked shaking his head. "She told me we're just friends."

"But you left the bar with her?"

"I was having a really bad day and she offered me some nonsexual comfort."

"So you didn't have sex?"

"Not even a little."

"Great," she said with a smile. Relief flooded over her face. "Wanna take this somewhere more comfortable?"

"Are you, ya know, sober enough for this?"

"Oh yeah," she laughed. "I wouldn't say no to a drink though."

He wondered how many alcoholics would say "no" to a drink right after falling off the wagon.

She waved at the lady in the Uber and opened the back door. She grabbed a messenger bag out of the back. "We're all set thanks for waiting!"

"Sure thing, Hon." The woman said with a scowl. "Did I hear gunshots?"

"Firecrackers," Zurik said with a smile. The woman nodded, but it was obvious she didn't believe a word of it.

"Leave your car," he said. "I'll drive, we can pick it up in the morning."

She slid her hand back out of the bag, keys in hand and unlocked the cuffs, tucking them in the back pocket of her jeans.

"If you're a psychopath, just remember Paul saw us together and he's a great cop."

"If I wanted to kill you, you'd be dead already."

"That wasn't creepy at all."

"It was supposed to be reassuring—not sure where I went wrong."

"Probably the part where you said I'd be dead."

"Well, I don't want to kill you or you to be dead," Zurik said looking her in the eye. "This town needs cops like you."

He placed a hand on her bicep for sincerity. She looked at him with those brown eyes.

"Alright, let's go." She said biting her lip.

Morgan watched Zurik as he drove. Something inside her was like a horny teenager again. She placed her hand on his knee and slid it up his leg. A smile broke his serious demeanor and she wondered what he had to be serious about. They stopped the bad guys, saved the victims, and best of all? Zurik wasn't a killer so she was free to give in to her deepest desires where he was concerned. She couldn't even remember the last time she'd had sex.

Zurik let go of the shifter and slid her hand up further. She smiled as she felt how excited he was at the idea of them going to bed together. She leaned into him, placing her head on his shoulder and he rested his head on hers. Her heart soared.

He picked his head up and downshifted as he turned into a driveway just off campus. The white house needed a new coat of paint and some of the dark blue shutters were falling off. Home repair wasn't at the top of Zurik's list apparently.

He hopped out of the car and jogged over to her side and opened the door. She took the hand he offered and lead her up the walkway to the front porch. He opened the door and she tilted her head.

"No lock?"

"Nope," he gave a weak smile.

"Just hold that thought while I clear your house," she reached for her gun.

"Hold on," he slid a hand around her waist and pulled her close. "It's OK, Trent probably just ran to the store."

"Giving the guy who's been creeping around the perfect opportunity to sneak in and set up cameras or take up residence in your attic."

He placed a finger on her lips and heat flooded her veins. His touch was like magic. Setting every piece of her a light with a burning need. He slid his hand over her face to cup the back of her head before capturing her lips with his. He nipped her lip and then kissed a burning trail down her neck. She pushed her body against his. He was like a solid wall perfect tawny flesh and muscle. He pulled her inside and shut the door. She leaned back against the door and slid the deadbolt into the locked position.

"Where's your bed?" she asked not realizing she was out of breath until she heard her own voice.

"Right this way," he said as he grabbed her ass and lifted her up. She wrapped herself around him. She couldn't remember the last time a man carried her. If a man ever carried her. He made it seem easy as he walked up the stairs. He went to the door at the end of the hall to the left. She flicked the light switch on as he closed the door.

His room was on the smaller side. A full-sized mattress lay on the floor in the middle with several guitars and amps on stands around the room. There was a desk that was piled high with clothes, guitar pics, and music but nothing typical of a desk.

He laid her down on the bed and laid himself between her legs. He paused with one finger in the waistband of her jeans. So close to where she wanted his touch the most, yet so far away.

"Are you sure about this?"

"Yes," she moaned. He slid his hand along the material, his finger sliding along the tender flesh between her hips. "Wait."

He froze looking up at her.

"You don't like--have anything do you?"

"No," he said. "Do you?"

"No."

"Alright then," he unbuttoned her jeans.

"Condom?"

"They're in the bedside table, I figured I'd—loosen you up a bit first."

"You mean oral?"

"Yes," he nodded.

"Oh OK," she put her head back and took deep calming breaths. He unzipped her pants so slowly. It was almost like he wanted her to freak out and stop him. She needed this. Needed him to touch her. They had a big win tonight and she was going to celebrate, dammit.

He pulled her jeans off and tossed them behind him. He slid his hands up her thighs and she shuddered in anticipation.

His hands gripped her hips and then paused. After a moment she opened an eye and looked at him. He was staring disapprovingly at her.

"What?"

"You look like you're about to get your teeth drilled."

"I haven't done this in a while OK?" she put her head down and took a deep breath trying to calm herself.

"Are you 100% sure this is what you want?" he asked crawling up the bed to lay next to her. She opened her eyes to look at him. He was gorgeous. Even with those creepy electric blue eyes. Yes, this was what she wanted.

"Yes I am, I'm just having trouble getting my body to cooperate."

He gave a heavy sigh and cupped her cheek with his hand. She gave a light smile and he moved his hand down her body. With a feather-light touch, he moved down her neck, between her breasts, and toward her hips, raising goosebumps the whole way.

Just when she was sure he was going to slide those magic fingers between her legs he reversed directions. When he reached her neck, he buried his hand in her hair and pulled her to him for a fierce kiss. She deepened the kiss, pressing her body into his and pulling at his clothes. He pulled away long enough to remove his shirt and settle in between her thighs. He moved to kiss her but she stopped him. She took in his body. He was as ripped as he felt under his shirt but he was also covered in scars. Some looked like bullet wounds, others like knife wounds, and burns.

"Holy shit," she pushed him back so she could really take it in. "What happened to you?"

He ran a hand through his raven hair. "I've been doing this a long time."

"This? Hunting non-human things?"

"Yeah," rolled back to lie down next to her. "Since I was a teen."

"You're kidding," she turned to look at him more. "Did you have help? An adult to keep you safe?"

"Lex when he was home. My Grandfather didn't want me to do it so he thought ignoring it was the best way to stop me."

"That worked out."

"Clearly." He rolled onto his stomach and started fiddling with his fingers. "Look I don't like to talk about my past. I'm not one to wallow or seek pity."

"Zurik—"

"I'm gonna hit the shower." He jumped out of bed and grabbed a folded towel off the dresser by the bathroom door.

She flopped back on the bed wondering if someone so damaged could ever be normal. If his body looked like that, what would his mind look like? What would his heart look like if she could see those scars?

She sat up, listening to the water turn on and the sounds of Zurik washing. Maybe it was the alcohol or maybe it was something deep within her desperate to connect with another person, but she stood, grabbed a towel off the dresser and pushed her way into the bathroom.

# NOT MINE

Morgan stood in the bathroom watching Zurik. The water ran down his back like the caress she was dying to give. The tile on the floor was warm and inviting. She removed her shirt and opened the glass to the shower.

Zurik looked over his shoulder. Surprised to see her. "I don't want to talk about it."

She fought back a smile. The stereotypical tough guy. He likely had some serious issues lurking under that tawny flesh. But right now, they both had an itch and she intended to scratch it. She reached around him to grab his shaft. It was hard and ready. Velvety soft. She pressed her body against him sliding her other hand up his back as she played with him.

"Who said anything about talking?" she asked with an impish smile.

He turned to look at her. Unsure. He was like a wild beast. She had to work to gain his trust but she had a feeling it would be worth it in the end.

He brought his face down to hers, capturing her lips as he pushed her back against the shower wall. He rained kisses down on her, his hands slid over her body making her shudder and moan.

He picked her up and she could feel his hardness pressing against her.

"Condom!" She shouted. He growled and put his head to her chest. Still carrying her he left the shower and placed her on the vanity, the cool marble made her yelp.

"Sorry," he said picking her up and placing a towel underneath her. He pulled a condom out of the vanity drawer and slipped it on. She spread her legs and leaned back. "Are you sure?"

"Yes, Zurik, please." She stared him in the eye as she said it. He slid himself inside her and she jumped. He filled her to the point of pain. "Wait."

He paused while she adjusted to his size. He slid his thumb over her cheek looking for signs of pain on her face. "Let me know when you're ready. Or we could stop."

"I'm starting to feel like it's you who doesn't want to have sex with me." She laughed.

"Some women aren't as strong as you Jen. I don't want to hurt someone because they didn't think they had another choice."

She smiled. She rocked her hips against him and they both moaned in pleasure. He moved his hips against her as he scooped her up off the vanity. She clung to his shoulder using the leverage of his hips to move up and down his shaft.

"You feel so good," he whispered in her ear as he carried her back into the warm shower. He leaned one arm against the shower wall to steady them as he started thrusting into her. She moved with his rhythm to heighten their pleasure. The heat in her core built and built until she was ready to burst.

"I think I'm going to come," she said breathlessly.

"Do it, I want to feel you come," he whispered in her ear. That pushed her over the edge. Her body shuddered with her orgasm and she pulled him close. He quickened his pace and joined her in the moment of pleasure. She could feel him pulsing inside her. He put her down and stepped back to lean against the stone wall of the shower. He slipped the condom off and opened the door to the shower to toss it in the trash before rejoining her. Under the water. He turned a knob on the wall and the second shower turned on. Giving them more than enough water and room.

"That was nice," she said feeling sleepy and leaning against the stone.

"I still want to taste you," he said indignantly.

"You will."

"I will?"

"I haven't had an orgasm in years and I have an addictive personality," she laughed.

"Years?" he gasped.

"Yeah," she answered not willing to get into it further. She stepped out of the shower and grabbed her towel. "Where's the booze you promised?"

"In my bedside table."

"With the condoms?" she said in faux surprise.

"It made sense at the time you know, indulging in one usually leads to needing the other."

"Apparently it goes either way," she called out as she opened the bedside table. A handgun, a box of Magnums, and an assortment of nips. "You're better stocked than the liquor store."

"Well, you never know what a woman's preference will be."

"How many women do you sleep with on average?" She asked opening a nip of fireball and letting the burning cinnamon distract her from how nervous she was about his answer.

"Depends." He said laying down on the bed. She tossed him a tiny bottle of rum.

"On?"

"If I've had a bad week. If the bad guy got away."

"What if you kill the bad guy and save the girl?" she looked around. "Do you have ice cream?"

"If I kill the bad guy the high usually gets me through."

"So you use sex to cope?" she asked smiling as she found a rolled up bag of chips.

"Those are from yesterday and yeah you could say that."

"What about love and all that noise? Don't you want that?"

"I did once," he rolled onto his back gifting her with the view of his naked body.

"And now?" it was like prying information from a brick wall.

"Now not so much."

She gave a heavy sigh and decided to wait to push any further.

"What were those things we fought tonight?" She asked picking through the chip bag looking for the folded over ones.

"Those were Fey. As in Morgan Le Fay, Arthur and the knights of the round table."

"Why are they kidnapping women?"

"A few hundred years ago Morgan went missing. Some hunters think she's dead, others say she's just hiding out gaining strength. Some say she found her people mistreating women so she cursed them and vanished. But whatever the reason, when she disappeared, her people only had male offspring. So they started mixing with humans. Most women don't want anything to do with the half breeds though. You noticed the sandpaper skin, pointed teeth, and cat's eyes right?"

"Yeah, less than fuckable to say the least."

"So they kidnap young women and teens and force them to birth the next generation. I've been hunting Dominick and his kin for years. I thought this year I'd have him. But he was gone before the fighting even started."

"What else is there?" she asked as the reality of the night finally hit her.

"A lot. I'll get into it with you more later. For now, we need to get some sleep. The fey will be out in force tomorrow night. They need to collect all their women and impregnate them by the full moon."

"Why?"

"It's a magic thing, Trent could explain it to you. I stopped paying attention as soon as I realized there was a deadline."

"You're bad to the bone aren't you. Don't listen in class, don't obey the law," she shook her head while making a tsk sound with her tongue.

"What can I say? The chicks dig it."

Morgan woke with a stretch. Her eyes clenched shut when she heard the crinkle of a chip bag as she shifted her body. Then her hand grazed warm soft flesh. Her eyes flew open as she leaped off the bed and last night came rushing back to her. Zurik was sound asleep, snoring softly. One of the Fireballnips she'd had was teetering dangerously on the edge of the bed. She lunged to catch it but missed. It hit the wood floor with a loud clink and skittered across the room. She eyed Zurik. He didn't appear to be awake. Until her gaze reached his face. One blue eye glared at her.

"Sorry," she whispered unsure who else in the house might be sleeping.

"It's fine, I always get four hours of sleep." The sarcasm was plain as he rolled onto his back. She looked away. "We're shy now?"

"I shouldn't be here," she said searching for her clothes.

"Why not?"

"Because you're a suspect and I'm an officer of the law— unless I get fired."

"You know I didn't do it," he offered, tossing her shirt. She pulled it on over her head, wondering if the Captain would feel the same way. She'd left the damn crime scene with him. How could she be so stupid?

"I don't think that will matter to my boss." She gave wry smile. "You've been a thorn in his side for a very long time."

"While protecting the people of Starsboro."

"He doesn't know that and I don't think I can tell him."

"I'd rather you didn't." Zurik sat up and pulled her jeans out from between the bed and the wall. "Most people don't handle it as well as you did."

She paused. Why wasn't she freaking out? This is freaky stuff and yet she felt fine.

"I don't think it's really hit me yet. Tell me a vampire is in town and I might lose my shit."

"Vampires don't exist," he said. "The legend was made up to help the Fey get through life. Of course, the ridiculously beautiful part isn't true anymore."

Morgan nodded looking around the room. "Any idea where my underwear ended up?"

He leaned over the bed, looking at the floor, he held up a pink thong with a smile.

"Not mine," she said, her lips thinned as she stared at the tiny piece of clothing. He frowned and tossed it to the side before continuing his search.

# TEN
# BROKEN PROMISES

Morgan pulled into the police station underwear-less and hungover. She'd been suspended for yelling at Zurik, but now that she was at the scene with him where the victims were found, she'd have to face the music. There was no way Cavazos could cover that up, and she wouldn't want him too.

She walked into the station. Cavazos walked up to her but Captain Reynolds cleared his throat to signal he'd be going first.

She gave Cavazos a small smile before crossing the short distance to the Captain's office.

"What part of suspended didn't you understand?" He asked. His tone was full of frustration and disappointment.

"Captain, I—"

"What part of stay away from D'Vordi did you not understand?"

She crossed her arms over her chest and flopped into the chair. This was meant to be a lecture, there was no point in even trying to justify her actions to him.

He paced back and forth rubbing his temples as if trying to relieve a headache.

"We found all the missing women." He finally said as he sat down on the edge of his desk. "Because of you."

She looked up from the hangnail she'd been picking at. "Excuse me?"

"You were drinking weren't you?"[1] he gave a heavy sigh. She looked away from him again as her cheeks began to burn. "I don't know what to do with you, Jen. I promised your old man I'd look out for you. Keep you on the straight and narrow."

"I'm fine," she snapped. "He hasn't been sober in twenty years, I have one drink after two years of sobriety and everyone is freaking out. Well, guess what? I still caught the bad guys."

"No, you didn't. The perpetrators were gone by the time we got there." He eyed her. "If you'd been sober, we might be having a different conversation right now."

"If I was sober I wouldn't have approached Zurik in the bar, I certainly wouldn't have gotten in his car and dropped pins for Cavazos. And I wouldn't have overheard him get the call about the van. Last night would have one more boring night where the victims stayed locked up and we were left without another clue if I'd been sober."

"Do you really believe you needed alcohol to solve this case?"

She paused. Was that what she was saying? "No, but I needed alcohol to solve it last night."

"I disagree." Reynolds leaned forward to look her in the eye. "I think you would have followed Zurik, from the safety of your own vehicle, and made all the same discoveries. But the bad guys would be in a cell right now.

Not off looking for new victims or hiding out until the heat dies down."

"I guess we'll never know," she stood and headed for the door.

"Your suspension continues until further notice. I need to review this case. I'll let you know if you still have a job on Monday."

She gripped the door handle, her knuckles turned white as she stood there taking everything in.

"Don't take another drink, Morgan. If you do, you're done in this station. Go to a meeting and use the time to get yourself back on track."

She nodded before leaving. Cavazos was waiting by her desk with a cup of the putrid station house coffee.

"Morgan I need to talk to you," He said as she walked passed him.

"I can't talk just now Cavazos, can I call you later?"

"It really can't wait." He followed behind her still holding the coffee. "I'm worried about you."

"Why? I already got the speech about my drinking Paul, I really don't need another one."

"No, not that. I mean that's concerning but you've pulled yourself out of that before I think you can do it again. I'm talking about your relationship with D'Vordi."

She stopped just short of her car in the lot. "Excuse me?"

"You left with him last night and since you drove your car here this morning and you don't have any friends outside of the station, I'm thinking you didn't go home last night."

Ugh, she hated detectives. "So?"

"So he's a suspect in multiple cases. I'm worried about you Morgan. About your job and your well being."

"Thank you for your concern Paul, now if you don't mind, I really need to go contemplate the meaning of life in relation to alcohol and maybe hit up an AA meeting."

She got in her car, slammed it into reverse, and peeled out of her spot. Why was everyone treating her like a child? She was a grown woman, making her own choices. Maybe drinking wasn't the best decision but she didn't want to give Zurik up. But she couldn't tell Cavazos he was just a monster fighter. He'd think she'd gone mad and then she'd lose her job for sure.

Zurik left the house feeling pretty good about the day ahead. He'd check in on Misty in the hospital, get any information she might have about the fey's habits and meet up with Morgan later for some hunting and maybe another night of passion. Now that he'd had a taste of the detective, he couldn't get enough.

His phone buzzed in his pocket. He pulled it out to check the ID. Jocelyn's name and photo flashed across the scene. She was probably already at the hospital.

"Hey Jo, I'm on my way," he said with a smile.

"Jo can't come to the phone right now," the male voice was sinister and all too familiar.

"What did you do, Dominick?" he asked masking the anger bubbling up in his chest.

"I couldn't help myself. She's just so—supple. Perfect for bearing lots of children."

"If you hurt her, I will kill you. Slow and painful."

"I have no doubt," the lightness of his tone and slight chuckle in the words made Zurik's blood run cold. "So I'll give you a choice, bring the lady cop to me and you can have your beloved Jo back. Refuse and Jo will be mine. My son's need brides but this one is just too perfect."

"When and where?" Zurik snapped.

"The old bridge on Hadley at dusk," he chuckled. "And Zurik, don't be late. I might change my mind."

Zurik hung up the phone and suppressed the urge to throw it with everything he had. Jo was innocent in all this. He couldn't let her suffer for his mistakes. He should have been out there hunting last night. Not banging the hot detective. Now he had to choose. Morgan or Jocelyn.

Morgan was pacing in the kitchen wishing she had a bottle of Jack when her doorbell rang. She padded to the entryway to find Zurik on the other side of the door. She opened it.

"You need to go away I'm trying really hard not to drink right now," she said with a smile.

He slid a hand around her waist and pulled her against him. Familiar heat filled her at his nearness. He captured her lips with his. The kiss was fierce, needy, and desperate. He pulled back his eyes filled with sadness.

"I'm sorry about this," he said as she pushed his way inside. "Get your shoes on."

"Why?" she asked grabbing her sneakers, sitting down to put them on.

"They got Jocelyn."

"Oh my god," she moved faster. "What do you know?"

"They'll be at the old Hadley Bridge at sundown. And they're willing to trade her for—you."

"Ok so what's the play?" she asked as she stood up. He put a small silver knife in her hand.

"Once Jo is safe I'll come back for you," he said.

"What?"

"This blade is silver it'll hurt them. Just hold them off till I can get back."

"How is this a plan?" she snapped as he grabbed her arm and walked her outside. She scrambled to grab her keys and lock up the front door.

"It's all I've got, you can handle yourself."

"Yes I can but you never give the kidnappers what they want! Haven't you ever seen any movie? Like ever? That hostage negotiation 101."

"Morgan," he rubbed his eyes. "I'm not asking you."

"This is why you'll never be happy," she seethed. "You hurt the people around you."

"That may be right, but Jo is worse off with them than you would be. And right now, that's what I need to focus on."

"Zurik, I'm not going with you if you don't come up with a significantly better plan."

He grabbed her arm and walked her towards his car. "I told you, I'm not asking."

Panic flooded her veins and as the realization of what was happening hit her. She gripped the knife in her hand and jabbed it into his stomach. The blade bent on his abs and cut her hand.

"What the hell?" she snapped.

He gave her a pained look. "I work out. Now let's go."

"No, I'm not going with you! You're being stupid and you're going to get me killed!"

He looked away from her and grabbed her wrist. Dragging her to his car he tossed her in the trunk with ease. She slammed her fists on the metal and screamed. The trunk opened and Zurik pulled some duct tape off a roll.

"No, you don't!" She screamed. She grabbed a crowbar from beside her and hit him in the head. He grabbed it and pulled it out of her hands. Tossing it aside he tied her hands together and put tape over her mouth. How was he so strong?

She screamed through the tape even if no one else heard her at least Zurik might feel bad. If he could feel anything at all.

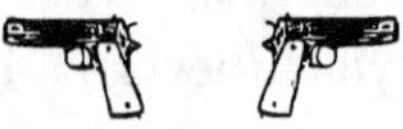

Zurik pushed Morgan onto the old bridge. She glared at his roughness. He looked miserable but she didn't care. He was an asshole. She really knew how to pick em.

"Your prize awaits," Zurik shouted into the mist. "Give me back mine."

Jocelyn fell into view as if she'd been shoved. She also glared at her attacker.

"Perfect." Dominick stepped out of the darkness behind Jo. His eyes hungry with lust. Morgan felt sick watching him. "It's a shame though."

"Come on, Jo," Zurik said. She looked to her captor and then ran to Zurik. He took her in his arms and hugged her close. He could care, just not about Morgan. He nuzzled her, breathing in her scent before whispering in her ear.

She nodded as she looked at him. Tears filled her eyes but she fought them back glancing at Morgan. She hesitated. Morgan shook her head. Jocelyn was innocent in this. She shouldn't feel guilty about how things were going.

"Run!" Zurik shouted. She took off through the woods. Morgan's heart raced at Zurik's booming voice and the next item on the agenda.

"She truly is gorgeous," Dominick said looking at Morgan. "Have you had her as well?"

Zurik looked away then glared at his foe.

"You have!" he laughed. "And you're giving her up? Maybe I chose the wrong whore."

"It doesn't matter who you choose," Zurik said. "Because I'm going to kill you long before you're able to hurt anyone else."

"It's a pity really," Dominick said ignoring Zurik's promise. Morgan smiled as hope filled her. Maybe Zurik wasn't going to just leave her to the psychopath after all. "I mean I still have three sons without brides. Since you took them all."

"May I recommend Tinder?" Zurik said with a smirk. "But you have to let them go home after, so it might be a bit an adjustment for you. Your sons are young, I bet they'll catch on quick."

"They won't need too." The fey's smile sent a feeling of dread through Morgan's chest, releasing adrenaline through her body all over again. "They can share your girl. You know those hips well. She'll bear them many children."

Zurik looked over his shoulder to where Jo vanished into the darkness of the trees.

"You'll have to be very fast if you want to save her."

Zurik looked at Morgan. Her eyes wide with shock. This was why they needed a better plan! He pulled the gun out of the waistband of his pants and tossed it to her as he ran after Jo. "Aim for the heart!"

Morgan looked at the gun in her still duct-taped hands then to the fey.

*Fuck.*

# ELEVEN
## RESCUE?

Jo flew through the woods. She knew this path better than the back of her hand. She'd run it a thousand times as part of her morning routine. Her eyes scanned for the Camaro. If not for the phone call she'd promised to make, she would have run straight back to her dorm. She rounded the corner and her heart scored as the trademark musclecar slid into view.

Her foot was yanked out from underneath her and she fell to the ground. Something dragged her backward, sliding over the cool dark earth despite her struggles to move toward the car. She rolled over and pulled at the cord around her leg. Her gaze followed the thin rope to one of her captors. The smile spreading over his lips sent a shiver down her spine. Two more stepped out of the shadows. Three against one.

"No," she yelled.

"Yes," he yanked the cord back, pulling her with it. She fought to get free as the cord dug into her ankle.

"No!" she was screaming now. Thrashing wildly, not caring about the damage to her ankle. The rope went limp as the fey's head hit the ground and turned to dust. She looked up to see Zurik and relief poured from her eyes. The look on his face was lethal as he targeted the next fey. He lifted his machete and pulled back. She turned her attention to her ankle. Freeing herself, she ran for the car. Then it hit her.

"Where's the cop?" she shouted as Zurik grabbed another fey by the hair.

"Back on the bridge," he said as a woman came up behind him and slammed a log into his head.

Zurik fell to the ground. Clutching his head.

"Stay away from my children!" she shouted.

Zurik stood up. "Teach your children not to kidnap and rape women and they won't have a problem with me!"

"I do, they only did what their father asked of them."

"Teach them when to say no to daddy then."

"He'd kill us." Her voice was hollow with fear and shock.

"If you leave now and I never see you again. Then you can live."

Jocelyn's breath caught. Zurik never let anything go. No matter how harmless. She turned and limped toward him her ankle starting to swell.

"Fine, you'll never see us again."

"Mom," one of the men hissed.

"Shut up Jason, or die here and now," she growled. He stayed silent. She turned back to Zurik. "You have my word."

"If I hear about any women going missing, I will hunt you down and kill all three of you."

"We understand," she said herding the two young men away.

Zurik stood tall watching them go. As soon they were out of sight he looked to Jocelyn. "Keep up." Before she could ask what he meant, he bolted for the bridge at full speed. She ran after him as best she could on her injured ankle.

Morgan faced the man on the other side of the bridge. His smile sinister and his light blue eye sent an eery chill down her spine. She fought the duct tape on her wrists and he strode forward.

"I'm going to keep you all to myself." He said licking his lips. She couldn't get a good grip on the gun with her hands tied. She aimed it at him. "It's too bad Zurik got to taste you. Anything I hold over the little bastards head is a bonus for me. I know it's petty, but he's killed many of my children over the years. A few of my brides too."

Morgan's heart sank. He killed the victims?

She squeezed the trigger and the recoil of the gun pulled it straight out of her hands. She looked to the fey, he was looking at a shoulder wound. Shit, she'd missed!

"You are a feisty one," he smiled his pointed teeth glinting in the moonlight.

She lunged for the gun but he caught her by the bicep and hauled her to her feet. She struggled but his grip held fast. He ripped the tape off her mouth. A yelp escaped her control at the pain of the adhesive coming loose.

"I'm really quite surprised he brought you to me. He seemed rather attached last night."

"What do you mean?" she asked not wanting to give him the psychological advantage.

"When you kissed him outside our home. His eyes lit up. He wanted you bad. And seeing as you didn't pick up your car from the bar until this morning I'd say he got what he wanted. All he wanted from you clearly."

Morgan glared at him even as pain filled her chest. Why did she care? It was one night. It meant nothing to either of them. It was fine. She slammed her knee into her captor's groin and fell to the ground as he crumpled beneath the blow. She scrambled to her feet as he coughed and groaned. She was nearly to the darkness of the woods when a hand slid into her hair and yanked her backward off her feet.

"Some wives require a beating or two," his voice was strained as he dragged her back across the bridge. "I suspect you'll need a few extra."

"You'll have to kill me," she snapped. "I'll never let you touch me."

"You say that now, but I've been training women for hundreds of years. I'll break you just like I broke all the rest."

Rage filled her chest. She grabbed his hand where he held her hair and twisted her body to face him locking his arm straight. She forced her head up breaking his hold on her. Before she could leverage her freedom, he punched her hard in the face. Pain spread across her cheek into her nose and eyes making it hard to breath and see. He kicked the side of her knee, smashing the joint. She screamed out as the pain ripped through her leg. He followed up with a punch to her stomach, knocking the wind out of her. She fought back the bile that rose in her throat as she fell to her knees. He kicked her in the ribs lifting her off the ground. She felt her ribs snap against the pressure. He wound up for a second blow but something tackled him to the ground. Zurik was on top of him raining blows down on him like a crazed UFC fighter.

Jocelyn hobbled after him running straight for Morgan.

"There's a knife in my back pocket!" Morgan shouted as Jocelyn reached her.

Jo pulled out the mangled blade and frowned. "What the hell happened to it?"

"I stabbed Zurik," Morgan answered with a hard stare.

"Oh, OK," Jo nodded as she used the blade cut the edge of the tape so she could rip it open. As soon as her hands were free Morgan lunged for the gun, her ribs and knee screaming in protest.

Morgan watched as Zurik swung his machete at the fey's neck but the fiend took a quick step back out of range. Dominick stepped forward landing a punch to Zurik's stomach. Zurik fought to breath as the air rushed from his lungs. He delivered an uppercut to the fey's chin. And kicked his chest, pushing him back over the edge of the bridge. Zurik grabbed his wrist as he teetered on the edge. The rushing water from the falls was deafening. The sound of the gunshot muted by the raging water. Dominick slipped from Zurik's grasp into the mist.

Zurik looked back to Jocelyn and Morgan. Morgan let the gun fall to the bridge as she the darkness started to close in.

"Did she get him?" Jo asked as Zurik picked up his gun and slid his hands under Morgan's back and knees.

"Yeah," he said. "She got him."

Morgan let the darkness take her.

Morgan woke up the next morning in a hospital bed. She tried to sit up but was quickly reminded by a shooting pain that her hand and a few ribs were broken. A full cast covered her leg, her ribs screamed as she tried to breathe, and her hand was in a brace. Her left eye was swollen shut and a dull ache radiated from her cheek. Flowers and balloons that said, "Thank You!!" and "Get Well Soon!" filled the room, but those were not what surprised her.

Slumped in a chair in the corner by her bed, was Zurik, his leather jacket slung over him like a blanket.

A light knock sounded on the door before a nurse snuck in. Her pink scrub pants and floral top were decidedly cheerful.

"Oh, you're awake," she said with a smile. "Are you ready for more pain meds?"

Morgan nodded. "Has he been here all night?"

"All night and most of the day, ma'am," she responded quietly. "You've been in an' out for the last sixteen hours. He has not left your side." She left the room; Morgan assumed to get the medicine.

When the door opened again, there was a large, older nurse with the one who had just been in. The younger one had a tray with syringes and cups with pills. She went straight to the IV to administer the pain medicine, scanning the barcode attached to Morgan's wrist and then each bit of medicine. The larger nurse held a clipboard and looked like she might be about to ask insurance questions.

"I am here to help you," she said. Her name tag read, 'Jackie.' "If you are in any danger at home, tell me now, sweetie. I can help you."

Morgan frowned and pain lanced through her face. She lived with an ornery feline who she was mildly allergic to, but she wasn't in any danger. The nurse looked pointedly at Zurik. Morgan followed her gaze and understanding hit her harder than Dominick had. She burst out laughing. Despite the tremendous pain, she could not stop but did manage to calm it down to a chuckle.

Zurik sat up at the noise and smiled at her. God, he was gorgeous. Even after fighting the forces of darkness for half the night and spending the other half in a hospital room.

"How are you feeling?" he asked. The nurse slipped her card into Morgan's good hand and left the room.

"I'm fine," she replied, still smiling at the nurse's assumption.

"Fine?" He laughed. "You can take one hell of a beating."

The other nurse looked concerned now.

"I need to speak to my captain," she told the nurse. "I have to fill out a report on the kidnappers."

"He was notified when you woke up." She gave Zurik a wide berth. "He should be here soon. Do you want me to wait with you until he gets here?"

"Will you people stop it?" Morgan laughed. "Zurik did not do this to me. He just found me and the kidnap victim and brought us here."

"Well," Zurik said, "Jocelyn insisted on going home."

Morgan shrugged. "I would have, too. I get it."

The nurse left as Captain Reynolds entered. He glared at Zurik before turning his attention to Morgan.

"Do you remember what happened?"

"I got a call from the kidnapper. He wanted to meet at the old Hadley Bridge," she started.

"Why didn't you call for back up?"

"Someone's life was in danger, Captain. I made a call."

"You went against protocol. You are lucky to be alive."

"I am," she agreed. "But Jocelyn is safe, and that makes it worth it."

"I want your report on my desk by the end of the week." He gave a heavy sigh. "Your suspension will continue, with pay, until I make a final decision. I need to know that I can trust you to make the right decisions when I'm not around. Look at **yourself**Morgan. 'Someone' could still be alive if you'd made a different call."

Reynolds left the room. Taking her hope with him.

"Morgan," Zurik said, standing.

"Don't," she said as pain welled up in her chest, and not from her broken ribs. "You made the wrong call and I might lose my job for it. If you'd taken two seconds and listened to me, I might not be in the hospital. I'll cover for your ass because now I know what's out there but we are not friends and I don't need you here protecting me. I'd like to be alone."

He nodded and leaned down, kissing her forehead. A large part of her wanted to pull him into bed with her and snuggle him close. But he'd betrayed her. He'd let his own stupid bullshit put her and Jo in danger. She couldn't let that slide. No matter how good he was in bed. Or how much sadness lurked in those electric blue eyes.

"If you need anything," he said, holding her cell phone out to her, "don't hesitate to call."

He looked around the room and then slipped a handgun from his waistband and put it on her bed. "Just in case."

She took it and nodded. As soon as the door closed behind him, she let out a sob. She tried to stay quiet; it was too painful, so she let it all out.

# TWELVE
# GUN SHOTS AND HOSPITAL GOWNS

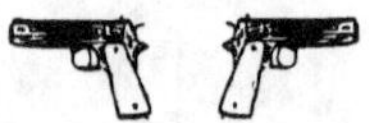

Morgan lay in bed, her cheeks tight with dried tears. The door clicked open and she heard someone yelling for help in the hall.

"Go away Zurik," she said rolling over as gingerly as she could. "I don't want to talk about it now. Maybe not ever."

"But I've come so far?" the voice slid over her like a bad dream. She turned to look over her shoulder and there stood Dominick.

"I—I—killed you!" she gasped trying to get to the nurses call button. He ripped the cord out of her hand and tossed it to the floor.

"You killed my brother bitch, and now you're all mine. I'm not obsessed with reproducing like he was. I'm just in it for the kill."

He grabbed her throat as she struggled cold metal touched her bare leg. *Zurik's gun!*

She slid her hand under the blankets and grabbed the gun and aimed it at his chest through the blanket.

Just as she was squeezing the trigger, a machete went through his neck like butter. The Fey turned to dust as the gun fired right into Zurik's shoulder.

"Son-of-a-bitch!" he shouted, pulling the gun out of Morgan's hand and tucked it under her pillow and slid his jacket on.

The door flung open and the floral nurse rushed inside. "Did I just hear a gunshot?"

"No," they said in unison.

"There's gunshots in this hospital?" Zurik said in shock. "I think we should move you to Jacksonville."

"Yeah I heard a strange sound too but I'm not sure it was a gunshot." Morgan offered. "And I think I'd know. Also, Probably not the best idea to rush into a room you think there was a gunshot in."

"I have to check on other **patients**," she said visibly shaken. "Are you sure you're alright Ms. Morgan?"

"Detective, and yes, I'm fine."

The door slid closed slowly behind her.

"Oh my god!" Morgan said pulling him to her and yanking at his coat.

"Ouch!" he snapped. "It's not like there's a **wound under** there or anything!"

"I can't believe I shot you! I've never shot anyone I didn't mean to shoot before."

"Well that's comforting," he laughed. As she tried to see the wound but his shirt wouldn't allow it.

The door opened again and Morgan froze until she recognized Trent.

"Did I hear a **gunshot**?" he whispered angrily.

"She shot me," Zurik said pointing to his shoulder.

"Well, good for her, what about the fey?" Trent asked trying to see his brothers shoulder.

"I feel so loved."

"The fey is gone, can you grab some gauze? And Zurik, take off your shirt." Morgan ordered.

"She just wants to get me naked." Zurik smiled.

"Shut up!" Trent and Morgan said in unison.

Zurik glared at them and pulled his shirt over his head.

"Well if you had to get shot, this was the place to do it," Trent said as he pushed gauze to the wound. Zurik hissed at the pain.

"Did it come out the back?" Morgan asked, leaning in the bed to see for herself. Her ribs protested but she needed to know how badly she'd injured him.

Trent looked at the back and shook his head. "Sorry brother, this is going to hurt."

"Why aren't you pre-med again?" Zurik asked. "I'd kill for a bottle of—anything right now."

"Because the shiny equipment and sterile workspaces would freak me out. I'm too used to dingy lit kitchens and patients that are awake."

Trent dug around in the drawers for a few minutes but came up empty-handed.

"What?" Morgan asked.

"Nothing to grab the bullet with. We're going to have to wait until we get home."

"Grab some of the sterile stuff." Zurik barked.

"You're really going to do it yourself? There's a hospital full of professionals."

Trent gave Zurik a hard stare. "If she's sticking around she needs to know."

"I'll meet you in the car," he said. Then he grabbed Trent by the arm. "Your car, we'll come back for mine once I'm done bleeding."

"I packed the wound with gauze you're not gonna bleed on anyone's car."

"**Your car**."

"Fine," he threw his hands up as he left the room.

"Are you good?" Zurik asked.

"Depends, were they twins or triplets?" Morgan said with a sarcastic laugh.

"Twins I think."

"I'm sorry I shot you."

"I gave you the gun to use it. I just thought you'd use it on the bad guys."

"Zurik, you were the bad guy." Her voice was strained. "You kidnapped me, tied me up, tossed me in the trunk of your car and gave me to the devil."

"And you shot me," he said with a weak smile. "We're even."

She gave him a hard stare.

"Look, I didn't mean to actually give you to him. I should have had a plan for if he went after Jo."

"You would have if you'd actually included me in any of the decision-making process. I'm a cop, I know what I'm doing in situations like that. I could have helped you."

"I know that. I'm sorry."

"Was there something you'd like to tell me?" she asked pointedly.

"Get some rest. It can wait."

Morgan sat at her desk in the precinct watching the detectives around her. They hustled in and out, leading suspects and victims to interview rooms. Solving cases and making a difference in the world.

She used to feel like she made a difference. But knowing what was out there, she found herself wondering, had she really made a difference? She glanced at the Captain's office and found his brown eyes locked on her. He motioned for her to join him. Grabbing her crutches she hobbled the ten feet to his door.

"You're not the first one of my detectives to realize there's more to protecting and serving than putting away human monsters." He said as he shut the door. He walked over to his desk and pulled a bottle of scotch and a glass out of the bottom drawer. "You are the first to jump into D'Vordi's bed though."

"What, or who, I do in my personal time is none—"

"Easy," he spoke over her outrage and put a hand up. "I'm not judging you. I'm trying to offer you a job."

She frowned. "I have a job—don't I?"

"If you quit drinking, you can have your job back and you can go back to the way things were. Closing normal cases and tossing the not normal ones to your new—friend. Or you can stay on the payroll, but work with D'Vordi and M'Kray. Help them. Offer them the resources we have. Databases, interdepartmental communications, back up when needed. You'll be the scourge of the office. They'll call you everything from

Buffy to Moulder. But you'll be making a difference in this town. A big difference."

She stared at the bottle of scotch. "And if I can't quit drinking?"

"If you don't quit drinking it won't be because you can't," he looked at the bottle. "It'll be because you don't want to. And if you are doing the thing I'm asking you to do, I can't make you give up the comfort found at the bottom of a bottle."

She swallowed hard. The fey must be the tip of the supernatural iceberg. "When do I have to let you know by?"

"When you come back to official duty, I'll expect your answer."

She took a deep breath and her ribs screamed destroying any hope she'd had for a calming effect.

"I can't trust Zurik." She said.

"Before you get too set in that way of thinking, you should read this," he tossed a file across the desk to her. She opened it and saw the photos of a much younger Zurik holding a young woman. He was clutching her to his chest. Her hair was soaked in blood and there was a body on the ground behind him.

"What is this?"

"Zurik's high school girlfriend. She died. Killed by something I still can't explain." He shuddered. "That's why he hasn't been locked up yet. I know everything. He doesn't trust me though."

"Why?"

"Because I told him her death was his fault. It wasn't exactly, but if she'd never gotten involved with him, she'd probably still be alive. And I was young. Naive."

"And you want me to what? Be buddy-buddy with him?"

"You can handle yourself."

"Clearly." She snapped holding up her crutches. "He gave me to that—thing."

"He saved Jocelyn. And he went back for you. I'm not saying you should trust him. I'm saying you should work with him." He pointed to the file. "And this knowledge is the tool you need to keep yourself safe while doing it.

She looked at the case file on the table. Turned the page to see photos of officers ripping the girl's body from Zurik's arms. His eyes looked—red?

"What's with this photo?" she asked pointing to Zurik's eyes.

"He's not human Morgan." Reynolds took a long pull of the scotch bottle. "The FBI and I, want you to find out what he is. And report back. For now, he's on our side and that's great. But when he loses it, when he's the one we're fighting, we need to know what he is and how to beat him."

"You want me to spy on him?" she didn't like this. Not at all. She shook her head. "I can't do that."

"Morgan, this information could save lives."

"I can't." She said. "I won't."

He leaned forward and flipped to the next photo in the file. Zurik's teeth were elongated, and his eyes were completely blood red. There was something black around his eyes as he threw a police officer with ease.

He turned to the next photo, Zurik going after another officer. The last photo was Trent, no older than fourteen, pulling his brother off the officer, Zurik's eyes were returning to normal.

"I'm not spying. But if things go south with him, I'll do what needs to be done."

She paused on her way out of the office, turning back to look at him over her shoulder. "Was it you?"

He frowned. "Pardon?"

"Did you mess with the tape of Zurik killing the fey?"

He gave a heavy sigh, the hint of a smile at the edges of his lips.

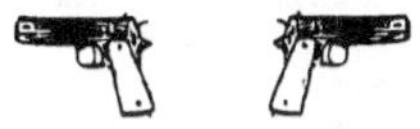

Morgan sat on her couch, Game of Thrones on the TV, and her cat Jim, a blue tiger, snuggled on her lap. Her cast-covered leg stretched out on the couch with her crutches near the coffee table, one lay on the floor.

A knock sounded on the door and the Jim shot to his feet before giving a back curling stretch and yawn.

Morgan leaned over the couch to see who was there. One jean-clad leg and a tattooed arm could be seen in the window next to the door.

She huffed as she retrieved her crutches and another knock sounded.

"Just a minute!" she snapped. Hobbling to the door she opened it to see both D'Vordi brothers. She thought about slamming the door shut, but then paused. Reynolds' words rung in her head. She stepped aside, letting them in. Zurik brushed past her Trent slipped past politely adding a mumbled 'thanks'.

"How's your shoulder?" She asked crossing her arms over her chest.

"Better," Zurik said.

"Look we thought we should come and talk to you. I mean it's not every day you discover there's otherworldly creatures hunting women in your town." Trent offered.

"I don't know if now is the right time," she answered. "I'm not in a good place. I don't know if I can go back to my job or if my job will even be there when I get back on my feet. And will I be able to function as a police officer knowing what I know? There's still too much up in the air."

"Well," Zurik said as he reached down to scratch Jim's head. "When you're ready you know where to find us."

"Thanks," she said. She had her hand on the doorknob when another knock sounded. "What the hell?"

She peeked through the side window. No one was there.

"Please, I just knock to be polite." The female voice came from directly behind her. Sending a chill down her spine. Before she could turn, Zurik grabbed her by her arm and yanked her towards him. Pain ripped through her body. She turned her head to see a woman in an empire waist green and gold gown, with long dark hair and emerald eyes. Morgan's crutches lay on the floor by the woman's feet, she leaned against the couch for support. "You killed two of my children, mortal."

"Morgan La Fey," Trent said looking at Zurik.

"I've killed plenty of your children before and you've never shown up." Zurik spat. The woman's eyes shifted from Morgan to Trent and then landed on Zurik.

"Aren't you full of magic. Oh my." Her voice held the excitement of a child on Christmas morning. "What are you?"

Zurik looked at Trent. His body tensed and he bounced on the balls of his feet. "Nothing you haven't seen before."

"Something about you is familiar. Your energy reminds me of—Merlin." She came to the realization as she spoke it. "I have to have a taste."

"Excuse me?" Zurik said. Before anyone could react, she vanished, then Zurik did too. They reappeared across the house, Morgan Le Fay's arm wrapped around Zurik's chest from behind. She sunk her teeth into his neck, drinking his blood. Trent leapt over the couch, grabbing a lamp on his way and smashed it over her head. She pulled back, blood still flowing from Zurik's neck as La Fay licked her lips, unfazed by the lamp. When she opened her eyes, they glowed blood red.

A deep laugh emanated from her belly. "Oh, you are a special treat."

Trent grabbed the poker from the fireplace and moved to stab her. She vanished and the poker was embedded in the drywall instead.

"What the fuck was that?" Morgan asked. She hobbled over to Zurik, grabbing her sweatshirt from its place on the back of the couch and put it on his neck.

"I don't know," Zurik said.

"Morgan Le Fay is supposed to be dead. Long dead. For the last hundred years at least." Trent said as he pulled the poker out of the wall. "She was supposed to have been the last witch burned at the stake."

"I'm thinking she could have escaped that situation pretty easily," Morgan said. "So Arthur, Merlin, Lancelot, that's all real?"

"Most of it, it's still a story but it's based on more realistic origins than some historians believe," Trent said.

"And you?" Morgan asked as she pulled the sweatshirt from Zurik's neck. The bite was already starting to heal. "What are you?"

# How to Diagnose a Changeling

Doctor Rachel Donahue sat on her couch looking at her son, Jacob's baby pictures. She ran her hand over the plastic-covered photos as love swelled in her heart at his chubby cheeks. She could almost hear his precious belly laugh. He never laughed anymore.

A few weeks ago everything had changed. First with the car accident that had killed her husband and partner of nearly ten years and now…. She couldn't even bear to think about it. *I wasn't prepared to lose Tomas; I'm just being irrational. It's just stress*, she thought.

She glanced down at the smiling baby in the photos, and a sob escaped her control. Her hand flew to her mouth to silence it. She stared, eyes wide, at the hallway, fear replacing her sadness. After a moment, she thought she might be safe and dared to take a deep, silent breath. Then she heard it. The small padding of tiny footy-pajama-clad feet marching down the hallway. It was dark. The only light was from a small lamp that sat next to her, but the kitchen window allowed a soft blue glow to backlight the tiny figure. She fought the urge to run and hide. Two red eyes shone above his head, and panic started to fill her. She closed her eyes, and when she opened them again, the eyes were gone, and the light in the hall was on, illuminating her child.

"Mommy?" His tiny voice was so similar and yet there was something off about it, something that urged her to cry out, to scream. "Can I sleep with you, Mommy?"

"Sure, baby," she forced herself to say. She lay down and turned out the light by the couch. He ran over to her, throwing his tiny arms out. His smile was so pure. For a moment she lost herself in it and felt joy like she thought she would never feel again. As they snuggled though, reality returned to her. This was not the real Jacob. That thought was not what terrified her. It wasn't what kept her up at night or what haunted her dreams.

*I am powerless to find my son. They would lock me up as soon as I tried to get help. Where is my baby?*

In *How to Get Kicked Out of School*, Trent is front and center. While Zurik and Morgan are off fighting a would-be demon in Charlotte (*How to Make a Monster*), Trent finds himself face to face with a real demon in Starsboro. Not to mention the girl he has feelings for and her crazy ex's plot to get them kicked out of school.

Read *How to Get Kicked Out of School* for free at

**CameronQuinnBooks.com/freebook**

# ONE
# DEMONS AND GENTLEMEN

Lindsey shot up in bed with a scream. She searched the darkness for anything familiar. Her gaze settled on the window. Moonlight poured into her bedroom. She ran one shaky hand through her thick blonde curls. As her breathing and heart rate slowed, she looked toward the end of her bed and jumped. Three men stood there. They were the pale, almost see-through like most of the ghosts who visited her. They wore blood-soaked bandages and were so thin she could see every bone that wasn't covered. Their eyes were sunken black holes.

She knew what they wanted. She grimaced at the thought of giving it. Reluctantly, Lindsey held her hand out to them. As soon as their ghostly fingers touched her, she felt the pain of their death. It coursed through her with a vengeance. She doubled over with the cramps only someone who has truly starved could understand, and she felt sores cover her skin. They were everywhere and completely unyielding as she screamed. Once it passed she lay in bed, sweating and spent from the pain.

"You can go to the light now," she said without looking at the men. "I will tell your story."

Her anonymous blog, telling of her ghostly encounters, seemed to help other mediums as much as it helped the ghosts. Technology might be a time suck but in this case, it was a win-win.

It took a few minutes for her to have the strength to open her eyes. When she did, the room was completely empty. She gave a sigh. Being a medium was difficult. Physically helping trapped souls pass on was harder. The deep thump of the bass from the party next door vibrated through her room. There was no way she would be able to go back to sleep. On top of the loud music, Lindsey felt gross. Getting up she slipped out of her pj's and donned her pink fuzzy robe.

Without another thought, she grabbed her shower caddy and headed out the door. As she stepped outside her dorm, she nearly collided with Tami, her roommate, and Tami's girlfriend, Kelsea.

"Did the party wake you?" Tami asked, concern creasing her deep brown brow. She wore a bright green tank top and jeans, and her dark curly hair was pulled back into a tight bun. She was a gymnast through and through.

"As hard as it is to believe, no." Lindsey laughed. "I had a nightmare and then…you know."

"You should join the party!" Tami said, either ignoring her statement or thinking that partying was literally the answer. Kelsey slipped past Lindsey into the dorm, no doubt to get the candles going. No one loved temperature play quite like Tami. "There are a ton of hot guys! It would be a shame to let them go to waste."

"Tami," Lindsey said, drawing out her next words. "You're a lesbian."

"Exactly!" she said. "Someone should be enjoying them!"

Lindsey laughed as she looked down the hallway to the men who had spilled into the hall. Maybe a quick tryst was what she needed. A headache started to grow in her temple and she gave a groan. "I think I just need a hot shower and some quiet."

"Trent D'Vordi is there." Tami's tone indicated she knew how much power that name held for Lindsey.

"He's cute," she played. "So, what?"

"Please, Girl. He is the hottest, nicest guy on this campus, and—I'd wager—any other." Tami dragged Lindsey down the hall to peer into the dorm full of party-goers. Sure enough, Trent sat on the countertop directly opposite the door. He was chatting up a few men she knew to be pre-law and looking incredibly sexy as usual.

"Trent's into the long-term thing, and I really don't need that right now."

"Lindsey, he is easily the hottest man I have ever seen. You two were made for sex," Tami argued.

"Tami," Lindsey strained the name. "You are a lesbian!"

"Yeah," Tami snapped. "I'm a vegetarian too, but who do you have pick out and cook your steak?"

Lindsey gave a resigned sigh. "You."

"Exactly." Tami gave a triumphant grin. "So shut up and give the guy a chance."

"After I shower," Lindsey answered.

"At least ten minutes."

"Yes, ma'am," Lindsey answered, sounding sullen as she walked the last few feet to the shower.

"I expect a full report in the morning!"

Trent glanced at his watch. It was nearly 2:30 AM and he had his ECON final in about six hours. He looked around for Zurik. His band had finished playing a few minutes ago but he wasn't helping the other members pack up. Instead, he was chatting up Charlene Harris in the corner.

"Zurik," Trent interrupted. "I'm heading home. Are you OK to drive?"

"I haven't even started yet," Zurik answered with a smile. "You want a ride?"

"No, you have fun. I could use the fresh air." Trent smiled to himself as he headed for the door. It was a familiar song and dance they had been perfecting since Zurik was old enough to party.

Trent nearly made it to the stairs when he heard a scream coming from the girls' bathrooms. Without thinking, he dashed inside. He found Lindsey Grant soaking wet and covered in soap suds, wrapping a towel around herself. "I'm sorry, I thought I heard a scream."

She twirled around and he saw the fear in her green eyes. "You did! A woman needs help--she's being mugged behind the building!"

Without thinking, Trent turned on his heels and ran for the stairwell. He was outside in a matter of minutes, but what he found as he rounded the last corner to the back of the building was not a mugging. The attacker's face was contorted as he bit the woman's neck. Trent slammed into them. The creature went one way and the woman the other. Trent ripped his overshirt and put the cloth to the woman's throat as she nodded her thanks.

"You hunters are all the same," the creature hissed. His face appeared normal now. Normal and familiar. Trent stood between him and the woman. "I will kill you, as I killed the last. You can't make a difference in this world, little prince."

"Even if I only save one life, it's worth it." Even Trent was surprised by the conviction in his tone.

"If only, if only," the creature said lyrically. Trent stared, unable to place where he'd seen him before. He watched as the creature faded into nothing.

"Holy shit!" A group of partiers, who looked like they were about to have a smoke, stood behind Trent. "I must have taken too many mushrooms."

"Can you call the police?" Trent asked. One girl already had her phone out. "I need to follow him."

It was a lie, but he didn't want to be on the police's radar. Morgan was proof they didn't always listen to orders, and as fun, as she was to have around, other cops might not see things the way she did.

Once he was sure the woman was being taken care of and the paramedics were on the way he headed back up to the girl's bathroom. He looked away from the stalls as he entered.

"Did you make it…in time?" Lindsey asked. He stared at the door. He didn't know why they insisted on painting bathrooms salmon. No matter how new or clean, salmon always looked dingy.

"Yeah, she should be fine," he answered. "The paramedics are on their way."

"You can turn around. The room is designed for privacy."

Taking a deep breath, he turned. She was up against the stall door so all he could see was her shoulders. Still, knowing she was naked back there was more than he could handle. As he walked over to her he thought about the last time he'd seen a woman naked. It was close to a year ago.

"Thank you, Trent," she said, breaking his train of thought. "No one--usually when--no one listens."

"I need to ask you," he said. She looked at him with those large green eyes that almost looked brown because of the salmon walls. "How did you know she was in trouble? She was on the other side of the building."

"I know things...sometimes."

"How?" Trent regretted it as soon as he spoke. Who was he to pressure people about their secrets? "I'm sorry. I just...the mugger got away and I need to find him."

"Why?"

"He wasn't a mugger. But you already know that, don't you?"

"If I tell you something out of this world, do you promise to stay calm and not tell anyone?"

"Lindsey." He took a step toward her. "I have my own set of out of this world secrets. I won't tell anyone and I won't judge you."

Her lips thinned. She didn't believe him. She walked back under the water, where he could see her. He found his eye following the contours of her body, down her back to her round hips. She was curvy. She had hips he could grab onto. He felt his cock twitch and turned around, trying to focus on the issue on hand.

"I saw her being attacked."

He turned back to face her. "You--saw?"

"Yeah." She glanced at him over her shoulder. "I see things."

"Like--dead people?"

She glared. "I hate that movie."

"Am I right?"

"Yes, Trent," she snapped. "I see dead people. As well as other things."

"Like a mugging," he stated. "OK. How long have you seen things?"

"Forever." Something in her tone made him want to go to her. To comfort her. She turned around to face him and he quickly averted his gaze. He felt his cheeks flush as he studied the ceiling tiles. "Really?"

She started to laugh, and he had to fight the urge to look at her. "What's so funny?"

"You," she roared. Just as he thought he might lose the battle and look at her, a pair of warm wet hands grabbed his face and pulled him back in her direction. "If I didn't want you to see me naked, I wouldn't have let you come back in here until I was done showering."

"I just—I don't want to assume."

"I've had a hell of a night, and not in a good way. So I'm going to go back to bed, but Trent, thank you. For believing me."

She put her robe on and headed back to her dorm. He watched until she was safely inside. He ran a hand through his light brown hair and gave heavy sigh.

"Lindsey got you didn't she?" The voice belonged to a man leaving the party. He had messy brown hair and brown eyes that were a bit too far apart on either side of his, previously broken, nose. He had a crooked yet knowing smile as he looked back towards her door. "She's really special. If you can hold onto her, do it."

"What do you mean?" Trent asked.

"I'm Nick," he said, offering his hand. "I made the mistake of sleeping with her last term. She's not big on commitment. Which pretty much sucks for every guy who gets to know her."

"Thanks," Trent said, unsure how to respond. "But we just talked."

"Maybe you have a shot then." Nick wandered back into the party.

The walk home was peaceful. Few cars passed and no critters buzzed in the cold night air, giving him plenty of time to over analyze everything that Lindsey said to him and his every response.

"How to Abduct an Alien" is set in the Starsboro Chronicles Universe several years before Episode One.

When Zurik steps in to help an abductee, he finds an unlikely ally on the spaceship. Back on earth, however, his new friend finds himself on the examination table.

Plus three other science fiction shorts!

"How to Curse a Kingdom" is an epic fantasy story about Zurik and Trent's ancestor from their home dimension.

Pantheon outcast and god of war, Armon fears more rejection when he's called home to marry the goddess of creation and balance. But Demtrie accepts him--even without the disguise necessary for his former lover.

No sooner does he find happiness than he's plagued by the phantom cries of a baby. And the truth may curse the kingdom where he once found solace.

Plus three other epic fantasy stories!

# Want more of the Starsedge Universe?

The Nel Bently Books share a world with
The Starsboro Chronicles!

Sign up for V's Explorers to start the adventure for free!
https://dl.bookfunnel.com/78parc7q9k
Be sure to look for crossovers and Easter eggs.
Turn the page for a sneak peek!

# ONE

Vandalism across a perfect site was the best recipe for an archaeologist's worst day. Apparently, it wasn't enough that Nel Bently's visa had met with "authenticity issues" twice on her way into Chile. She ducked under the rope that had served as a barrier. *A poor one,* she mentally snarled. The site was a disaster. Great gouges carved the formerly pristine soil. The tools stacked under a tarp by the bushes were now scattered, bent and broken. What pits her crew had dug the week before were filled with rotting leaves and back dirt, the perfect, square walls of the trenches ruined and crushed in.

Nel stepped carefully through the mess. *This has Founders written all over it.* As a rule, Nel was a patron of locals and the people she studied. Coming onto culturally significant land, not matter how old the site, was always tricky and she respected that. The Founders were her exception. They took issue with any archaeologist that set boots near their land, despite admitting there was no spiritual or cultural significance to the sites Nel chose.

"Well, fuck." Her tanned hand raked sweat and sunscreen through her sandy hair. She had permits and this was blatant vandalism. She turned back to her colleague and the two grad students who had arrived early to help. They waited, uncertain, at the rope, tools and packs still held with earnest dedication. "Alright, Mikey, grab pictures of this mess. You two, packs and tools go there, and set up a tent over them. Once Mikey has his pictures, clean it up. Wear gloves, it's gross and smells like a sewer."

She watched as they moved to do her bidding, eyes wide as they got their first good look at the vandalism. "If you need anything, talk to Mikey. I'll be on the phone." She trudged up the rise, dry soil crunching under her battered boots as she tugged the satellite phone from its case in her pack. She dialed, listening to the clicks as the call connected and surveying the land below her. It was perfect, really. The site was nestled between a stream and the rise she stood on now. The water had carved deep enough to have been there when it was inhabited, but small enough to be on only the local maps. The rise, curving from the north to the west, was covered with artifacts. It was the first place they surveyed, and it provided natural protection from the wind that whipped off the Pacific, just a few hundred feet away.

"You've reached the machine of Dr. Martin de Santos. Leave your name and number and how I can help you, and I'll return your call at the earliest convenience."

"Martos, it's Nel. Site was vandalized, looks like Founders. We could use some extra help -- I don't know if my greens can handle this. Give my cell a call tonight, I'll be in town." As she hung up, she caught site of the rotted mess Mikey was about to shovel out. It was a rough shape of a symbol. "Oi! Mikey wait!" She snapped a few pictures with her handheld, before waving for him to continue and stamping down the rise. She had been unable to see it from the ground. It was the angled symbol with which the Founders signed their papers, websites and protests. As she watched the clean up, she noted two figures on the rise across the stream. Both wore telltale woven bands around their forearms. A cold mix of dread and defiance crawled down her spine. It wasn't like them to watch. *I'll be damned if I'm going to be cowed by radicals.* "C'mon," she called to the students, brown eyes fixed on the figures above. "I wanna see you moving dirt by ten!"

She returned to the site and sat on a rock, flipping through her field book. She had been digging since she was an undergrad. She had started with a history major, then steadily worked backwards in the time line, learning about anthropology, prehistorics, and paleolithics. She fell in love with her first dig. Now, with her doctorate defended, she had her own crew, her own research. Not to mention funding from a generous private patron to continue her passion for sweat, dirt, and work that made her body ache. She was staring at the page where she had sketched the site last summer when Mikey sauntered over.

He was a blocky man -- square head, square hands, square shoulders -- with only a slight paunch to round out the edges. "Sucks, eh? Think it was the Flounders?"

Nel smiled at his nickname for their adversaries. "More than likely. I tried to keep this site under wraps, but when you've grown up here, I think nothing escapes notice. They were watching us clean up this morning. Creeps me out a bit."

Mikey glanced at her, a frown crinkling his sun-weathered skin. Mikey was the resident prehistoric ceremonial specialist from their department, but more than that he was her best friend. "Everything OK?"

She shrugged. "I don't know." Her gaze was fixed on stain from rotted debris.

He rose with a groan. "I bet you a beer you pick up a shovel before tomorrow's over."

It was an old tradition. Nel could not keep her hands out the dirt, and even as site supervisor, she often found herself in a pit before long. She laughed. "You're on."

The Jeep ride back down to the village was about as comfortable as what Nel assumed a camel ride would feel like. The wheels bounced over a road that Class 6 trails in the U.S. dreamed of being when they grew up. It still made Nel feel decidedly badass. The trip took all of 30 minutes, though the distance was short, and it was close to 5:00 when they arrived. The house they rented for the summer -- Vecuna y Las Rosas -- was a small, narrow building, butted up against the hillside. A locked shed in the rear had enough room to park the Jeep and equipment, and that was all that mattered to Nel. She swung off the Wrangler's rollcage and began unloading.

"Go shower, get settled in if you didn't last night. Be downstairs in half an hour--I'm orienting the undergrads who arrived today. Dinner is whatever, wherever." When the students had scattered she felt Mikey's concerned gaze. She did not want that conversation. Not now.

"Meet you on the porch in twenty!" She hoisted her pack over her shoulder and grabbed the bag they used for the day's artifacts. She and Mikey had two of the singles on the fourth floor and with them the privilege of a private bathroom. The house was narrow and tall, giving the impression of precarious building. Nel knew it had survived every earthquake with minimal damage and had no qualms with her room at the very top. She dropped her field pack off in her room and spread out the finds on a desk in the spare room. Her fingers traced the artifacts. They were few, but promising.

Finally she grabbed her cooler and jogged down to the porch. Nel eased herself into a chair next to Mikey with a sigh. "What do you think this year'll bring?"

"Artifacts or crew?" Mikey popped open one of the precious ciders he shipped from the States.

"Crew. Artifacts are too close to home for me to comment on." The rest of the diggers arrived that afternoon. She wasn't looking forward to orientating a bunch of undergrads.

Mikey snorted, running fingers through his sweaty hair. "I think we'll get three partiers — old fashioned drunks — someone in a committed relationship and then the studious brown nose."

Nel laughed. "The usual round up?"

"Not every time. That one year everyone was a fucking introvert."

"You got a problem with that?"

"You kidding? That was the only year I got some decent sleep. Every other time it's either been drunkards stumbling up the stairs at 3:00 or someone boinking through the wall."

Nel raised her glass. "To introverts and celibates?"

Mikey hooted and tapped his bottle to hers. "Fuck yeah."

A door slammed above them and Nel smothered a smile. "I suppose I'll quiet down. They'll think I'm the partier among them."

Mikey laughed softly. "No, but you get a few beers and you'll be prowling the bars for a tanned-up senorita."

"She only chatted me up once, and it was my birthday." She leaned back with a smile. "You think she's still there?"

The screen door snapped open behind them and Mikey craned his neck to peer over. "Ahh, the crew approaches."

Four undergrads filed onto the porch. Each performed a rendition of the Where-Should-I-Sit dance before settling on the bench along the edge. Nel watched them shuffle about. She noticed more than a few puzzled glances directed at her and Mikey's un-showered appearance. *They'll be embracing dirty-beers soon enough.* A moment later her two grad students arrived and flopped, dirty, into the chairs.

When they stilled, she leaned forward, her eyes bouncing from one digger to the next. "Welcome to Chile. I'm Dr. Nel Bently and this is Dr. Michael Servais. We're heading up this year's field school for USNE. I know you all have to get settled in, you're welcome to skip dinner tonight. We do crew dinners every Wednesday. We'll get to know each other a bit now and the grad students will join us at the restaurant — Padradito's — a bit later. I know all of you by name, but you'll have to help me put faces to those names. Let's go around and introduce ourselves." The introductions were quick and awkward, Nel ignoring most of the innocuous why-I'm-an-arch-major nonsense as she tried to pin faces to names. *I'll learn about them over the next weeks. No sense wasting time now.*

When they finished, she polished off her beer and flipped open the cooler. "The social rules — I'll go over the work rules tomorrow on site — are simple. I know you're all of age, and we'll be drinking here, but try to keep the shenanigans to a minimum. Drink, but don't drive or be an asshole. Flirt with the local boys and girls, but don't get pregnant or knock someone up. Don't wander off alone. I don't have the budget for a drug lord's ransom, but that won't stop them from trying." The well-worn warning slid off her tongue and she added a narrow-eyed glare to the words. "Stay up late skinny dipping and bar hopping, but be out here on time in the morning. If you drink too much, you deserve the hangover." She made sure to punctuate the last statement with a heavy swig of her new bottle. "Now if you'll excuse me, I'm going to have a shower-beer."

The door clapped shut, muffling the stuttering conversation. She breathed a sigh of relief. She hated dealing with new people. She took advantage of the deserted upstairs by stripping off her dirt-logged clothes in the hall and almost skipping naked into the wet-bath. Within five minutes the solar-heated water ran red from the dirt ground into her skin.

Images of her vandalized site flashed through her mind. She slammed a fist against the tile. "Fuckers!" Her words echoed in the small room and she winced. There was no way Mikey didn't hear. The water was hotter than the day had been, and worked a few superficial knots from her back. *Man, there's nothing like a Phase II to screw up my back.* She stopped, soap forgotten in her hand. She had her own Phase II dig. Her excavation was fully funded by a third party and accredited through two universities. If under-grad-Nel saw her now she would never believe it. Nel tilted her head into the water with a happy sigh. Her mouth curled, eyes crinkling as they closed. *Someone pinch me, I'm dreaming.*


Continue Nel's adventure at:
**Books2read.com/travelers**

## About Cameron

Cameron J Quinn is the author of the award-winning series, The Starsboro Chronicles. She also dabbles in paranormal romance, thrillers, and science fiction.

When she's not writing fiction or wrangling her three children and/or her Marine veteran husband, she's working with authors to help them build successful careers as a Certified Book Launch Coach under her given name, Marissa Frosch.

She and her best friend co-founded Amphibian Press in 2014 and have been publishing books ever since.

**www.cameronquinnbooks.com**

www.ingramcontent.com/pod-product-compliance
Lightning Source LLC
Chambersburg PA
CBHW071018180726
48291CB00004B/1524